## THE RAID

The Comanches screamed and to[...] the animals. But a rampaging herd of cattle could rarely be headed off. While the Indians were occupied, Lige crept closer to Charlie. But when he came to within fifty feet, a tall bare-chested warrior stepped out toward him with a raised lance.

Lige froze. He fumbled with the ramrod and tried to find one of the paper cartridges Carol had handed him. He tore it open and poured the powder down the barrel. Then he rammed the ball home and slipped a fresh cap beneath the hammer. He cocked the rifle and prepared to fire. But his fingers were unable to move.

The Comanche hurled the lance into the ground in front of Lige and taunted him to come forward. Lige slipped around behind a tall oak. It seemed impossible the Indian could know he was there. Still the Comanche gestured wildly.

He knows I won't, Lige thought. He knows I don't want to die, not even to save my little brother. He knows I'm a coward. . . .

# THE RAID

*G. Clifton Wisler*

PUFFIN BOOKS

PUFFIN BOOKS
Published by the Penguin Group
Penguin Books USA Inc., 375 Hudson Street, New York, New York 10014, U.S.A.
Penguin Books Ltd, 27 Wrights Lane, London W8 5TZ, England
Penguin Books Australia Ltd, Ringwood, Victoria, Australia
Penguin Books Canada Ltd, 10 Alcorn Avenue, Toronto, Ontario, Canada M4V 3B2
Penguin Books (N.Z.) Ltd, 182-190 Wairau Road, Auckland 10, New Zealand

Penguin Books Ltd, Registered Offices: Harmondsworth, Middlesex, England

First published in the United States of America by Lodestar Books,
E. P. Dutton, 1985
Published in Puffin Books, 1994

3 5 7 9 10 8 6 4

THE LIBRARY OF CONGRESS HAS CATALOGED THE LODESTAR BOOKS EDITION AS FOLLOWS:
Wisler, G. Clifton.
The raid.
"Lodestar Books."
Summary: When his little brother is carried off by raiding
Comanches, fourteen-year-old Lige disguises himself as an Indian
and joins a former slave in a bold rescue attempt.
[1. Indians of North America—Captivities—Fiction.
2. Frontier and pioneer life—Fiction. 3. Afro-Americans—Fiction.] I. Title.
PZ7.W78033Ra 1985 [Fic] 85-10152 ISBN 0-525-67169-2

Puffin Books ISBN 0-14-036937-6

Printed in the United States of America

for my many friends at
Ben Jackson Middle School

# 1

The night was still, frozen in a kind of unearthly silence. Not so much as a breath of wind stirred the branches of the oak and locust trees that cluttered the rocky hillsides above the Trinity River. Overhead a thousand stars sparkled in the ebony sky, but only a sliver of moonlight illuminated the narrow trail ahead.

Lige frowned. The going had been difficult from the beginning. The trail was little more than a path, worn through the years by occasional travelers down from Buffalo Springs and the fords of the Red River farther north. A man on horseback might find his way easily enough in the daylight, but nightfall was another story altogether. Already

Lige's legs and shoulders were torn by the long jagged thorns of the locusts. He had grown weary, and his eyes half closed as he encouraged his tired mustang pony on down the trail.

"Come on, Skeeter," he whispered to the horse. "It can't be more'n a mile or so now. Can't be."

Lige blinked away the weariness from his eyes and tried to focus his attention on the bright yellow flicker of light on the distant horizon. It had to be the campfire, Zeke's campfire. No one else would make camp so far from the settlements, not in July, not with the Comanches raiding the northwest Texas frontier.

Lige shuddered. Exhaustion was taking its toll. His arms felt like iron bars, and his legs were limp, almost lifeless. He stared overhead at the stars. The dippers were there, well above the horizon.

That meant it must be past midnight. His father had taught him to use the stars as a clock. And it was only last April Lige'd sat with his brother Charlie beside a campfire out on the prairie past Decatur, picking out the constellations and listening to their father's stories.

It was hard to believe that was only three months before. It seemed like years, a lifetime.

Lige slowed his pony as he sensed a change in the terrain. The trail began meandering downhill, and the sound of crickets chirping all around him told Lige the river wasn't far away. A deer jumped out from his right, and he jerked himself upright in the saddle.

It wasn't like Lige to let something startle him like that. He knew this country, the Trinity and the rolling, untamed hills that lay beyond. But even the crickets seemed foreign, menacing. Every shadow seemed to hold danger. Lige's sweaty fingers gripped the reins tightly.

It was far different that June morning when he'd ridden with Charlie the twenty-five winding miles to his Uncle Henry's ranch. Lige had kept Skeeter trotting along at a brisk gait, stirring the dust of the trail so that more than once he imagined himself riding along on the crest of a cyclone. From time to time he'd hum some old song his older brothers Seth and Brad had passed along. That kept his mind off the ride, off the reasons he was being sent north to Uncle Henry while Brad and his father took their string of horses to market down south. Lige wasn't even being allowed to stay with his mother at the Harpers' place down the creek.

"Slow up a bit," Charlie would plead when Lige opened up too wide a gap between them. Lige would mumble something about eight-year-olds being poor traveling companions and slow the pace while his brother drew even.

"You'd think a boy who grew up around horses would learn to ride," Lige mumbled.

"You know so much 'bout horses, Lige, how come Papa didn't take you along to market this year?"

Charlie's words cut through Lige like a fresh-honed knife. Lige swallowed the pain that was filling his insides and stared ahead at the seemingly endless trail. It was impossible to reply. He knew no answer to that question, the one he asked himself almost every night.

The heat wasn't helping, either. Summer in Texas was like the inside of a furnace. It never really cooled off. The sun seemed to hang forever in the clear, cloudless skies, and what breeze there was vanished before noon and never reappeared before dusk. The only break came with rain, and it had been weeks since so much as a cloudburst had broken the monotony of the drought.

Once Lige had loved summer. His mama cut back on lessons, leaving time for swimming and fishing in the creek that ran along the boundary line of their ranch. His father let him run the horses, and he'd sometimes go hunting with Brad. Lately it had all changed. It seemed there was never an end to the work that had to be done. He noticed his father found little to smile about. And nothing Lige did satisfied him.

"Elijah, I wish just once you'd do a thing right," he'd say, shaking his head or kicking a rock across the barnyard.

He'd taken to using Lige's whole name, too, just like it was written in the family Bible. Lige hadn't been called Elijah since he was five years old. The first few times Lige just stood there, glancing around, half expecting some ancient prophet to be walking up the path from the creek. But prophets didn't make mistakes, and from the day Lige turned fourteen, he didn't seem capable of doing anything else.

"Papa's worried about things," Lige's brother Brad explained. "The market for horses is poor enough, and if it doesn't rain soon, we'll be lucky to manage enough hay to keep the stock fed this winter."

Lige knew that well enough. His father wasn't the only one who could worry. When Lige got upset, though, he only made more mistakes. His father would yell even louder. More than once Lige'd thought about signing on with the militia company at Fort Belknap, like Johnny Handley had. They only took boys sixteen and older, but Lige could stand tall, wear a couple of extra shirts, and pass for sixteen. Johnny'd done it.

Some boys his age had signed up to fight with Ben McCullough in Missouri, and one even went East, only to starve at Vicksburg.

"What use would the army have for a scraggly boy like you?" his father asked when Lige told him. "Elijah Andrews, soldier of fortune. The only use you ever had for a razor was to lance that boil summer before last."

Lige felt himself wither like a dying grapevine. His father laughed. Lige'd never considered it to be funny.

The very next week Lige's father had decided to send him to Uncle Henry's place up on the Trinity.

"Maybe he'll take you next time," Brad said as Lige led Skeeter out of the corral. "You'll be older. Taller, too."

"You were fourteen the first summer you went," Lige said, fighting to control the bitterness that was seeping into his voice. "I'm as tall as Todd Bonner, and he's been to Fort Worth twice this year."

"Be patient, Lige."

But Lige'd been patient. It didn't help much. No, to his father, Lige was about as much use as Charlie, so they were both being sent to Uncle Henry's. Two boys, fit for nothing more than chopping weeds and tending stables.

"You boys mind your Aunt Sally," Lige's mother said as he and Charlie climbed aboard their horses and readied themselves for the long trek north.

"Yes, ma'am," they told her.

"You watch out for your brother, Lige," his father said,

holding Skeeter's bridle a moment. "Don't cause your Uncle Henry any worry."

Lige nodded. He then took a long look at his mother, at the house that always seemed warm in winter and cool in summer. He waved to Brad, then turned Skeeter toward the trail.

Uncle Henry's ranch spread itself out over a dozen hills along a kind of horseshoe bend in the Trinity River. It was all that water that gave Uncle Henry a chance to run the herd of cattle and still plant a dozen acres in corn.

"That makes all the difference," Lige's father explained to him the first time they'd visited there. "Even in drought the Trinity has water."

More than once Lige had chased his brothers Seth and Brad across the muddy bottoms of the small creeks that cut his father's property. At best they were shallow streams in summer. Sometimes they were little better than a collection of stagnant pools.

Water.

Yes, water was life. You had a hard time finding a settlement more than a few miles from some branch of the Trinity or the Brazos. Lige didn't think more than a handful of white people had braved the wild buffalo valleys and open prairies farther west.

And there were the Indians, too. When Lige was seven or eight, the last of the Kiowas left the old Belknap Agency to cross into the Indian Nations north of the Red River. His father had brought horses for the army, and Lige had been taken along. The cavalry, all dandied up with a bugler and everything, had escorted them.

Watching the Indians had made him sad, though. They

were all herded together like horses, hauling what possessions they could manage in the backs of small wagons or on ponies. The old people lay in beds pulled along by horses. The women and children walked. The men rode spotted mustangs, but the animals seemed to lack energy.

Those Indians hadn't been very scary. Lige had a hard time getting frightened by Brad's stories of terrible raids to the north by those same Kiowas. The Comanches were another story. Some of them had never settled down to reservation life. Lige's own ranch had lost a few horses to them even before the war. When the fighting in the East started, the cavalry had vanished. Only a few militia occupied Fort Belknap. The Comanches got a little braver every month. Lately they'd been spotted down on the Clear Fork of the Brazos, up at the Jack County settlements, and even near Gainesville.

"That's another reason your father is afraid of taking you to the auction," Lige's mama had told him. "The Comanches would love nothing better than to steal two dozen of the finest horses in Wise County."

Lige'd smiled when she said that, knowing she wanted to make him feel better. But the truth was he'd never heard of Comanches stealing horses on the way to market. They usually sneaked in at night and stole them from under your nose. Actually, riding north to Uncle Henry's place with Charlie was much more dangerous. Lige's papa wouldn't have considered him brave for doing it, but a lot of the farmers who lived along the river had taken to riding in pairs.

Not that Lige was defenseless. He had Grandpa Clark's dragoon Colt, a cannon of a pistol the old man had carried during his last two years with the Rangers. That gun could blow a big hole in anything that got in range. When Lige shot a turkey with it in October, the recoil nearly knocked him to Arkansas.

Lige found it hard to be fearful. All his life he'd been riding up and down the creeks, through the hills, across the small farms that, like his family's, tried to scratch out a living from the rocky Texas soil. The jagged outcroppings of sandstone, the twisted limbs of the mesquites and junipers whose roots clawed away at the hard ground, the half-hidden springs that bubbled and flowed in the wet months and trickled in summer . . . they were all part of Lige's world.

He never kept track of how long it took to get to Uncle Henry's. The only watch he'd ever seen was owned by his cousin George. Aunt Sally had a small table clock in her kitchen, but long before Lige was born, sand and dust had gotten into its workings, and its hands were now frozen at two o'clock.

As Lige recalled, Mrs. Dickerson had been hanging out washing when he'd passed her place. Lige promised to send her regards to his aunt and agreed that the sermon preached by the Methodist circuit rider last week had been one of his best. Her daughter Muriel waved at him from the house, but Lige pretended not to see. Muriel was already half a head taller than Lige, and she wouldn't be thirteen till September.

After crossing the Trinity, Lige directed Skeeter down the narrow road that led to the trading posts at Red River Crossing. Skeeter appreciated the sandy surface of the road and responded with a rare nod of his head. Lige sometimes thought the horse could read his mind. They weren't far from their destination, and while that meant work for Lige,

Skeeter would get a cool drink from Uncle Henry's watering trough and all the grass he cared to eat.

"We almost there?" Charlie asked from his place five or six yards behind Lige.

"Just about," Lige said, sighing.

It was only a few minutes later that they galloped through the oak archway Uncle Henry and George had built the summer before the war. Soon Lige was rolling off Skeeter's side and leading the pony to the trough.

His cousin Carol emerged from the house to greet them. Her bright blue eyes sparkled, and a giant smile spread across her face. She swept back a stray strand of long blond hair from her forehead and danced down the steps to where Lige was standing.

"How about some mint tea?" she asked, producing almost by magic two tin glasses filled with a kind of tingly water and little sprigs of mint that grew near the garden. "Have a pleasant ride over?"

"Too hot and dusty," Charlie complained.

" 'Bout the same as usual," Lige told her after emptying the glass. "How've you been?"

"Fine. Glory had her foal," Carol said.

"Can I see?" Lige asked.

"I knew you'd be more interested in that horse than in me," she said, frowning.

Lige laughed. He and Carol left Charlie climbing around the porch swing while they walked to the corral.

Carol could only pretend to be hurt a moment or so. Lige smiled, and she couldn't help brightening. There was only a month's difference in their ages, and a sort of alliance had been formed by them years before. Until Charlie was born, they were the youngest in their families. She leaned against his shoulder, then steered him to the little filly that was following Glory around.

"Here, girl," Lige said, ducking under the fence rail and walking to the mare.

"I don't know how you do it," Carol said. "Glory hasn't let a soul near her."

"Magic," Lige said, stroking the horse's nose. "She remembers the grain I found for her last spring."

"I think it's because you smell like a horse," Carol said, laughing. "I guess I better get back to the house now. Mama has me sewing. You'll get to help with the shoeing."

"Then Zeke's here?" Lige asked, wondering how he could have failed to notice Zeke Jackson's wagon standing beside the horse barn.

Before Carol could answer, Lige was rushing across the farmyard.

Zeke Jackson was like no other man Lige had ever seen. He stood more than six feet tall, and his shoulders were rock hard and massive like the cliffs that towered over the Trinity at Harper's Bend. Lige once watched him lift the back of a wagon off the ground.

There was his blackness, too. Several of the families that lived along the river had black women to help with the kitchen work, pleasant people with sad eyes. Zeke's eyes were different, though. It was as if they were on fire.

"Well, I believe I see Lige Andrews," the man said as Lige trotted through the barn door.

Lige stopped beside the makeshift forge and struggled to catch his breath. He'd only imagined it was hot outside. The inside of the barn was stifling. Drops of sweat covered every inch of Zeke's exposed arms, and he constantly wiped his forehead as he hammered at the steel bar he would reshape into horseshoes.

"You'll want the horses brought in soon," Lige said, noticing the first set of shoes was near ready for fitting.

"Not for a while. Haven't seen you for a time. Seems you've grown some."

"A bit," Lige said as Zeke probed Lige's wiry shoulders with iron fingers.

"Thought maybe you'd be out ropin' horses this year. Or else takin' 'em to market." A heavy silence filled the barn, broken only by the heavy clang of Zeke's hammer. "Creek's full o' catfish," Zeke said between strokes. "James and Joe been takin' a barrelful most every day. Their mama'd rather have 'em at their chores, but boys got a right to fun come summer. You ought to get your share."

"I haven't had much time for fishing lately. Papa's kept me busy."

"A man can't spend all his time working, Lige. Got to have time for breathing."

Lige couldn't resist laughing. Zeke made life seem so simple. Sometimes Lige wished he could trade fathers for a time.

"Tough to do a lot of breathin' in this place," Lige said, coughing.

"Why don't you go see if you can scare up some more of those iron rods, Lige? There's not half enough here to make shoes for ten horses."

Lige walked back outside and found his cousin George busy tearing apart some old wagon wheels. Iron had always been hard to come by, but with the war, it was like gold. Old

horseshoes had to be reworked, and all kinds of metal imple-
ments were melted down to make shoes for the new string
of horses Uncle Henry added after rounding up wild mustangs from the distant hills.

George paused long enough to wipe the sweat from his
forehead. His broad shoulders were already their usual summer pink, splotched with clusters of freckles acquired gradu-
ally over their sixteen years, and bright yellow streaks were
beginning to appear in his unkempt mop of strawberry
blond hair.

George smiled out a welcome, shook Lige's hand, then
motioned to a wheel rim that was resting against the side of
the toolshed.

"Give me a hand with this," George said, handing Lige
the front half of the rim. George took the back, and they
hauled it into the barn. A half-dozen trips got the rest of the
metal transported.

"Now you bring those ponies in, Lige," Zeke said as he
finished shaping a second set of shoes.

Even though the little mustang ponies were broken to
saddle, they still tended to be skittish. But if you whispered
to them, tugged at their ears, and held them firmly, they
usually behaved.

"Still has the touch," Zeke said, taking the first pony
from Lige.

George stood in the doorway and smiled. "Never saw
anyone with Lige's way with horses," he said.

"You ought to tell Papa that," Lige said, watching Zeke
match a horseshoe with the pony's left forefoot. Soon the
blacksmith was hammering away, reshaping the shoe.

"He'll take you for sure next time," George told Lige. "Can't let it eat at you."

Lige sighed. He knew that was true, but he couldn't seem to help himself.

There was a commotion in the barnyard then, and a man in the makeshift uniform of a militia captain walked into the barn.

"You the smith?" the captain asked, staring hard at Zeke. Lige could tell they weren't going to get along. Zeke would never back away from anyone.

"Can we do something for you?" George asked.

"I need to have some irons put on a couple of captives," the captain said. "Can your boy over there do the work?"

Lige thought Zeke's eyes would burn right through the barn. But Zeke said nothing, just went on with the work.

George and the captain left, only to return a few minutes later with two Comanches. Lige stepped back and stared at the Indians. They were naked except for deerskin breech-clouts which hung from braided ropes around their waists. Their hands and feet were bound with ropes, and their eyes blazed defiantly.

They were nothing like the friendly Tonkawas and Caddos who scouted for the cavalry units before the war.

"Here's what we need," the captain told Zeke. "I've got ankle chains. All we need is to have them bolted."

A soldier held up the heavy chains for Zeke to see.

"I won't put chains on a man," Zeke said.

"You'll do as you're told," the captain said. "I never heard the like. My daddy used to whip his slaves."

"I'm no slave," Zeke objected.

13

George nodded, and the captain stepped back.

"You tell him this is a military command," the captain said.

"Zeke?" George asked.

"I come here to shoe horses, not chain men up like dogs," Zeke said. "You don't want my work, you tell me. But I don't make chains."

Lige's legs trembled as the captain set his jaw. Zeke wasn't about to yield, though, and Lige guessed the captain wasn't sure of his ground.

"I can do the job, cap'n," one of the soldiers said. "I seen it done before. You mind I use your forge?"

The question was addressed to George, who turned immediately to Zeke. The big smith nodded and stepped away. Lige felt his hands grow still. Zeke had finished shoeing the first of the mustangs, and Lige led the pony outside.

"No man should ever wear chains," Zeke mumbled as he joined Lige. "Ever."

"You can't tell what they did," Lige said. "Might've murdered some people."

"No matter what," Zeke said, his eyes colder and harder than Lige had ever seen them. "You know what it means to be a slave, Lige?"

"It means somebody owns you."

"Means you can't think, can't breathe, can't be."

"Were you a slave, Zeke?" Lige asked, half afraid of the answer.

"Once," he said as a sadness flooded his face. "I belonged to Mr. Henry Walker down to Waco. He had himself a cotton plantation, a big farm where slaves tend the fields. I run off twice before I'd seen ten summers."

"They shoot runaways, don't they?"

"Some. But slaves cost money. So instead they whipped me."

Zeke lifted his shirt, and Lige shuddered as he saw the great pink scars that remained from many lashings.

"Twice they put chains on me, Lige. Can't ever forget how they felt. Last time I swore never again. Then Mr. Henry went an' died. Dr. Sam got me in the will. He never held much with slavery, an' he gave me my freedom papers."

"I guess if he hadn't, you'd have run off again."

"Lige, I tell you this as a truth. A man'll run forever for a chance to be free. I'd rather be shot than chained up like those Indians."

Lige nodded his head somberly, and Zeke managed a smile.

"Chains, Lige, they take away your dignity. That's a big word, but a man can't live without dignity. You learn that, you'll be better for it."

That night Lige spread out his blankets in the soft straw of the barn loft, ten feet or so from where Charlie lay dozing in the darkness. Lige was still thinking about the scars on Zeke's back, about the darkness that filled those big brown eyes when Zeke had spoken about chains.

"Chains?" Lige whispered to the emptiness all around him. There were many kinds of chains. The worst kinds were the invisible ones that kept you imprisoned right where you were. Maybe that was why Johnny Handley had joined up with the militia—just to escape.

Papa will never understand about that, Lige told himself. And I'll never have the gumption to run off like Zeke did.

15

Lige swallowed the sob that was welling up inside him and sank into his blankets. Tomorrow would be another long summer day. And after it, would come another and another.

# 2

Lige was awakened by golden splinters of bright June sunlight creeping through the gaps in the oak planking of the barn. He sat up on his blankets and yawned.

Mornings always seemed to come earlier at Uncle Henry's. Already he could hear the chickens stirring in the coop. Carol would be down there gathering eggs for breakfast. He had little doubt chores were waiting for Charlie and him.

Lige turned to look at his little brother. Charlie was sprawled out all over the place, one leg on a rafter, an arm dangling off the ledge, straw blending in with his long blond hair so that it was difficult to judge where one started and the other left off.

17

"Come on, Charlie, time to get up," Lige said, shaking his brother's small shoulder not once, but three times.

"It can't be mornin'," Charlie moaned, standing up so that his nightshirt fell down past his knees.

"We'll be late for breakfast," Lige said, yawning again as he pulled on his trousers and felt around for his boots. "And chores."

"I'll eat your breakfast, and you can have my chores," Charlie said, scrambling into his clothes and ducking as Lige took a halfhearted swing at his head.

"That doesn't sound like much of a deal to me. Still, we ought to figure out some way to fatten you up a bit," Lige said, grabbing Charlie and squeezing his skinny arms. "I've seen nails with more fat on 'em."

"I wouldn't be sayin' a whole lot about that if I was you, Lige. I heard Ellie Nolan mistook a fence post for you and got splinters in her lip last week."

Lige managed to connect with a well-placed foot, sending Charlie head first into a pile of fresh hay. Charlie answered with a barrage of straw and a terrible scream. It was all Lige could do to keep from dying of laughter.

After declaring a truce, the two of them finished dressing and scurried down the wooden ladder.

"Never knew boys could sleep so late," Aunt Sally said as they approached the house. "You'd think they were raised in a city."

"Yesterday was a long day," Lige explained.

"You tell me when it's ever been different, Lige Andrews. Now you see if you can't fill my kindling box 'fore breakfast. Charlie, the pigs'll be hungry. Carol will have the buckets full by now."

"Trade?" Charlie asked, staring at the buckets of slop Carol was carrying around the side of the house.

"No, the pigs're all yours, little brother. Besides, you'd like as not cut your foot off tryin' to swing Uncle Henry's ax."

Charlie grumbled as he picked up the first slop bucket with both his hands and plodded off toward the sty. Lige followed Carol to the chopping block and prepared to start in on the wood.

"Papa's been talking about running the horses some," Carol told him as he took the first log and prepared to split it.

"You suppose he might let me run one or two of 'em?"

"Don't know. George was talking to him about it, though."

"That wouldn't be half bad. But it looked to me like there was still a lot of hay to get into the barn."

"That's not midday work, Lige."

"It is around our place."

Lige drove a wedge into the notch he'd cut in the log, then struck it with the back of the ax head so that the wedge began cracking the log in two.

"I'm glad you came again this year," Carol told him. "I know you're disappointed your papa didn't take you to the auctions at Fort Worth, but we'll have a fine time."

"I guess," Lige said, striking the wedge a heavy blow.

"Papa's been talking about us taking a basket of food and going up to the top of Jordan's Mountain. Maybe Sunday."

Lige tried to manage some enthusiasm, but it wasn't in him. Jordan's Mountain was little more than a tall hill, and

19

it wasn't much consolation for missing a trip to town. He hit the wedge again, and the log splintered.

"You sure can split wood," Carol said as Lige began slicing the two halves into kindling.

"Glad I'm good at somethin'."

"You're good at lots of things."

"Not to hear Papa tell it. I thought for sure he'd take me to the auction this year. He's always had two wranglers with him. When Seth went into the army, I just knew it'd be my turn."

Lige chopped away at the logs and tried to remember the day last February when Seth had put on his butternut uniform and ridden off to join the cavalry in Tennessee. Their mother had complained eighteen was too young for soldiering, but Seth had gone just the same. He was close to six foot and strong as an ox. No one would be telling Seth to go to Uncle Henry's for the summer.

"You still here, Lige?" Carol asked. "You haven't heard a thing I've been sayin', have you?"

Lige shook himself back to the present and shrugged his shoulders.

"I might as well talk to a wall. I'm goin' inside to help Mama set the table."

Lige wanted to say something, but the words shriveled up and died on his lips. He concentrated on the chopping instead. There was one thing that could be said for hard work like splitting kindling. It sure could take your mind off everything. And each time Lige brought the ax down, he felt like he was hitting back at something, at whatever it was that had been making his life so miserable of late.

"Everybody feels like that at fourteen," Brad had told

him. "That's a tough time to be alive. You get it over with, though."

But Lige couldn't remember Brad or Seth having such a rough time of it.

"That's more'n enough, honey," Aunt Sally said from the back door as Lige started to take another log off the pile. "Put it in my box and wash up, will you?"

"Yes, ma'am," Lige said, carrying the ax to the toolshed, then gathering up the kindling and filling the large wooden box beside the stove.

Lige joined George and Charlie at the washbasin. George went first, cleaning off bits of straw and stray milk from the morning milking. After Charlie scrubbed, Lige washed his own hands and took his customary place at the far end of the table. Uncle Henry gave thanks, and the family tore into the food.

"Worse than the pigs," Aunt Sally grumbled as the boys devoured the corn cakes and eggs, swallowed whole chunks in a single gulp, and poured glasses of cold milk down their throats. "Why couldn't the Lord've blessed me with a house full o' girls?"

"You know you don't mean that," George said between bites. "Why, who'd you have to sew and mend for?"

"To tell the truth, George Andrews, I've never been much on either one o' those."

"Who'd do all the work?" George asked.

"Carol does 'bout as much as I can get out of you," Uncle Henry said, winking at Lige and Charlie as George's face turned red. "An' girls draw boys like sunflowers draw bees."

Carol nudged Lige, and Aunt Sally coughed.

"There's youngsters present, Henry Andrews," the

woman complained. "I'll hear no such talk at my table."

"Beg your pardon, Mama," Uncle Henry said, bowing slightly to his wife. "Didn't mean to raise your dander."

"You just watch that tongue o' yours, Henry," Aunt Sally warned. "Mind you consider what that preacher said last week."

"Oh, I will, Mama," Uncle Henry said, winking again. "I wouldn't want to draw the fires of eternity down upon my head."

"I should think not."

After breakfast Lige followed George to the corral. After seeing the horses got fed, Lige led Glory and her foal out into the pasture while George worked with one of the mustangs Uncle Henry had rounded up that spring.

"You've got a natural touch with horses, Lige," Uncle Henry said as Lige stroked Glory's nose. "How'd you do with your papa's roundup?"

"I brought in four ponies," Lige declared proudly. "Like to have had a fifth, but it broke away at the last moment."

Lige remembered his father hollering about remembering to tie off the rope, being stupid and clumsy, and a hundred other things that chased the smile from his lips.

"We've got a lot of animals around here just now," Uncle Henry continued. "George can't exercise 'em all. You think you might could ride 'em down to the river and back a couple o' times each?"

"I think so, Uncle Henry."

"Well, when you get Glory put away, start with the bay."

"Yes, sir."

Exercising the horses was paradise to Lige. He was never

as at peace as when he was on horseback. He especially loved the mustangs. They never became entirely tame. It was that streak of wildness that set their feet upon the wind. Lige would hang on for dear life as they flew down the riverbed.

"I wonder if you wish you were still free?" he asked a brown-spotted stallion as he splashed through the shallows. "Do you feel like Zeke did, all chained up with no hope of escape?"

But the horse couldn't answer, and it didn't seem to mind the bit in its teeth or Lige's hundred or so pounds on its back.

"Want to help with this one awhile?" George asked when Lige returned.

"Sure," Lige said, climbing off the stallion's back and tying its reins to a nearby willow branch.

"What you do is hold him while I get on," George explained, handing over the rope to Lige. "Then you get clear."

"I know," Lige said, watching George gingerly mount a tall black stallion.

For a minute George seemed to be in complete control. Then the horse began kicking up its feet, snorting, and throwing up spirals of dust. Lige scampered away and dove under the fence.

"Bite his ear, George!" Lige hollered. "Hold on!"

But it was too late. George flew through the air and rolled into a heap beside the gate of the corral.

"Think I might ought to gentle him a bit more," George said, slapping the dust from his legs.

"Could be," Lige said, trying hard not to laugh.

George stripped off his shirt, threw it over a fence post,

and started back after the horse. Lige held the animal again, but George lasted no longer. The third time George seemed to get a better seat. As the horse went through its wild movements, Lige thought, I wish I could be more like George, more like Brad and Seth. George tumbled off the horse, only to get right back on. Lige wondered if he'd ever be like that himself. There was George, tall and straight as a white oak, with shoulders that could carry a sack of grain each. There was a confidence, too, about George, a determination that got him through things.

"I'll never be like that," Lige mumbled. Sometimes he wondered if he really belonged to the Andrews family. Maybe Lige was just some orphan abandoned on the trail, like Abner Sikes, brought up by strangers who needed an extra hand on the ranch.

"That's the craziest thing I ever heard," Brad had told him when Lige had mentioned it last April. "You look just like Mama. You've got her nose, her eyes."

But Lige wasn't sure. What could you tell about a person from a nose? As to eyes, half the county had brown eyes. It was Lige who had the wild, dark hair. Maybe it was his mother's hair, but Seth and Brad and Charlie were all as blond and fair as their father and Uncle Henry. George and Carol, too. During the summer Lige's shoulders would get leathery-hard and tanned as an Indian's.

"Better watch your scalp, boys," old Ernest Palmer had said one summer not long back. "That Lige Andrews is like as not to go on the warpath."

That had been funny at the time. It marked Lige as someone unique among the boys who lived along the creeks, reserved a special place for him in the raiding games they played during the summer. Lately, with news of Comanche raids on the Trinity and farther west among the Brazos ranches, it lost its humor.

You wouldn't make much of a Comanche, Lige Andrews, he told himself as he leaned against the corral fence. No, Lige wasn't the warrior type. He was more prone to doing figures or making up stories than dashing off on horseback to do battle with some deadly enemy.

Am I a coward? Lige had asked himself that more than once. But it wasn't something a person really knew about himself. Just suspecting it was enough to drive Lige half crazy.

"Seems to me we've got a boy here layin' down on the job," Uncle Henry said, squeezing Lige's shoulder and turning him around.

"I rode the horses, Uncle Henry," Lige said. "What now?"

"Boy must be simpleminded, George," Uncle Henry said, shaking his head. "I never knew a boy needed to be told what to do so much."

"You want me to start movin' the hay?" Lige asked, trembling as if waiting for an ax to fall on his head.

"Simpleminded?" Uncle Henry asked. "Downright addled, if you ask me."

"What then?" Lige pleaded, readying himself for one of the outbursts his father was given to unleashing lately.

"Well, Papa," George said, "if I was fourteen, dusty, and smelled like a barn . . . "

"Which you are," Uncle Henry said.

". . . I'd get myself down to Lodgepole Creek and see if I couldn't half drown myself before supper."

Lige stared as George and his uncle began laughing and slapping him on the back.

"Don't need to draw you a picture, do I?" Uncle Henry asked. "Get going."

"Yes, sir!" Lige yelled, racing off down the trail to the creek as if he were being chased by a bobcat.

Lige felt a little guilty as he neared the creek. He wanted to do something to show them all he wasn't a boy like Charlie, who spent all his time swimming and fishing and running around stirring up trouble. But he was tired, terribly weary from head to toe. The thought of plunging into the cold water took over.

"Yahhh!" Lige yelled, rushing over the hill that lay between him and the creek. As the branches of the oaks and willows flew by, scraping his legs and shoulders, he breathed in the wonderfully fresh summer air. He felt free. For a fraction of a second he was that Comanche warrior Ernest Palmer was always talking about, taking out after buffalo in the flat lands beyond the painted hills of the Palo Pinto Mountains. He topped the crest of the hill and slid into a pile of leaves.

It did feel good, just for a moment, didn't it? Lige asked himself. He sat there a minute smelling the damp grasses and willow trees all around him. Yes, the water would feel cool, refreshing, renewing. He couldn't wait to get in.

Lige made his way through an ocean of cattails to the bank. Just ahead a tall white oak tree leaned over a bend in the creek. A deep pool formed there, a perfect place for a morning swim. Most days Jimmy Henderson would be down there, splashing around with the Bailey boys, jumping out of the oak into the water. But they were nowhere to be seen. On the far bank, Joe and James Jackson were fishing from a small bluff. Lige waved to them, then sat down on a nearby boulder and peeled off his shirt.

Lige was always a little nervous spending time with the Jackson boys down at the creek. His mama didn't care for him to keep company with them, and he'd usually get a good talking-to if Aunt Sally or Uncle Henry saw him with them. He supposed it was partly because Zeke had been a slave. Part of it was their being black. But it was also because Lige had been born with a lazy streak, and his mother felt the Jackson boys only added to it.

"Those boys ought to help more with the farm," she'd said more than once. Well, maybe that was true. With Zeke on the trail, smithing at the ranches or repairing wheels or mending harness for the Overland Stage, his farm had mostly given way to brush. Lige's father and other men thought less of the Jacksons for that.

"Purely a waste," Mr. Bailey had said more than once. But in truth Lige thought they envied the way Zeke did what he wanted and got by. And Zeke wasn't above diving into the creek with his boys or racing horses with Doc Sam, betting two bits on the winner.

"Catfish gonna scare good if you jump in that creek, Lige Andrews!" James hollered.

Lige laughed. "Why, I'll just talk 'em into hoppin' onto the bank and savin' you the trouble of catchin' 'em," Lige said, kicking off his boots and shedding his trousers. "It's too hot for fishin'. Come on in."

Lige splashed into the shallows, allowing the brisk waters of the creek to envelop him. He sank his toes into the soft, sandy bottom and sighed.

"Water's just about perfect," Lige called out.

"Got to catch supper first, or Mama'll skin us like a pair of rabbits," Joe said.

"Oh?" Lige asked, raising an eyebrow. "Wouldn't want to keep you from serious work like fishing." Their mama was as apt to send them fishing as Lige's was to have him off climbing trees or chasing fireflies. Lige dipped underwater and vanished. A moment later he bobbed to the surface, holding a plump perch in his right hand.

"Would you look at that!" Joe said, standing up and shaking his head. "Next thing you know that boy'll be catchin' horses in his teeth."

Lige laughed with them. After tossing the fish to them, he swam over to the oak branch and pulled himself out of the water. He balanced himself carefully, then made a near perfect dive into the deepest stretch of the creek.

Lige splashed around by himself for half an hour or so, observing the Jackson boys pulling catfish out of the shallows and shouting back and forth. James was about ten, thin and quiet for the most part. Lige figured Joe to be close to his own age. Joe was a lot taller, though, with broad, blacksmith shoulders inherited, no doubt, from Zeke.

Suddenly there was a rapid movement through the trees. A horseman emerged just behind the Jacksons, and both boys dropped their poles and went flying into the creek.

"Haven't I taught you better'n that?" a voice bellowed. "Best to take your boots off 'fore jumpin' in a creek."

Lige laughed as he recognized the rider as Zeke Jackson.

"Daddy, you scared us half to death!" James protested as he searched for his fishing pole.

Joe just sat in the muddy bottom and laughed.

"Well, did you catch yourself a fish or two?" Zeke asked.

Joe produced a stringer with six catfish and Lige's perch. Zeke nodded, then slipped out of his sweaty overalls and jumped into the water beside his boys. Joe and James wriggled out of their clothes. Soon the whole creek was alive with their shouting and laughing.

"Well, Lige, you goin' to be sociable or just go on splashin' round by your own self?" Zeke asked.

"Oh, I thought I'd just go on splashin' around over here," Lige told them. The next thing he knew, Zeke charged like a bull buffalo, and Lige was buried by a mountain of water.

"I surrender," Lige pleaded, raising his arms.

"Well, I suppose we'd best let him live," Zeke said, smiling. "He is good to horses."

They all had a good laugh and spent another hour in the water. Finally, though, Lige's feet and hands became soggy, and he felt as if his whole body was waterlogged. He stumbled over to the bank and sprawled out in the soft meadow grass.

He sat there watching Zeke chase Joe and James around the shallows for a time. Then a chill began to wind its way through him, and he walked over to where he'd left his clothes and got dressed. As he picked up his left boot, he spotted something in the ground below. It appeared at first to be a sliver of rock, but when Lige washed it in the creek, he discovered it was a small arrowhead.

"Look here," Lige said, holding it up in the air for Zeke to see. "An arrowhead."

"Well, let's have ourselves a look," Zeke said, motioning Joe and James to the bank. The three of them gathered around Lige in the soft grass. Zeke then took the arrowhead and held it up to the sun.

"Hasn't been here too long," Zeke said, passing it around for the boys to examine. "See how sharp the edges are. They get worn after a time."

"There were Indians here," Lige said, glancing around at the oaks and willows as if they might be hiding a Comanche village.

"They might've camped right here," Zeke told them. "Weren't anything but red men in this country till thirty years or so ago. Caddos, maybe even Kiowas through here. Some Cherokees down from the Nations."

"I thought they'd be out west where the buffalo are," Lige said.

"Buffalo didn't always roam just there. Used to be all over the place. White men chased 'em west."

Lige felt all their eyes on him. It wasn't a comfortable feeling.

"I've seen Comanches through this country," Zeke explained. "They come down to find poles for their lodges."

"That's how this place got its name," Joe said. "From the time Mr. Bailey saw some Indians cuttin' poles here."

"I never heard about that," Lige said. "When was that?"

"Five, six years back," Zeke said. "They still come. It's hard to find anything up north or out west that grows straight enough for a lodgepole. Best ones are in East Texas. There's some tall timber in the Cherokee lands, but pitiful little where the Kiowas and Comanches make their camps."

"You been up there, Zeke?" Lige asked.

"Couple o' times. Tradin'. Mostly I stay to the south bank o' the Red River. Lot safer there."

James and Joe grinned, and Lige knew there'd probably been a hundred stories told around the supper fire about Zeke's adventures in the Nations.

"I guess they're welcome to a few trees," Lige said. "But I hope they don't get in a mind to take anything else."

"Me, too," Joe said. "Like my scalp."

"Hardly worth the effort," Zeke said, grabbing Joe and rubbing his head briskly. "'Sides, they value a white man's hair a lot more."

James laughed along with his brother and father, but it didn't amuse Lige much. The thought of having your scalp taken wasn't the kind of thing that made you sleep better at night.

"I'd just as soon they stayed to their side of the river," Lige finally said. "They signed a treaty."

"Oh, they signed all manner o' treaties, Lige," Zeke said, a hint of anger in his voice. "They owned it all, you know, every foot o' ground in this whole state. Then the Spanish came. Later on the Americans. Pretty soon people were gobblin' it up right an' left. The Indians fought awhile, then moved on along."

Zeke got to his feet then, and James and Joe joined him.

"Once you might've seen 'em right here, Lige, racin' ponies like you an' George do down the creekbed."

Lige closed his eyes and imagined he saw them, bare-chested and defiant like the two captives the militia had brought to the barn the day before.

"You suppose they'll come back here someday?" James asked. "Do you, Daddy?"

"Not likely, son. They've had their day."

Lige noticed there was a strange sadness in Zeke's voice

as he talked, almost as if those Indians were old friends and he missed them. Zeke passed the arrowhead back to Lige, then turned away.

"We'd best be headin' home now," Zeke announced. "Mary'll be wantin' to start supper 'fore long."

Lige nodded and began the short walk back to his uncle's house. There were still chores to be done before dinner, and he wanted to show George the arrowhead.

# 3

It was around noon the next day that the riders came, six grim-faced men carrying rifled muskets. They were led by Nathan Bailey, a tall Alabaman who'd come to the Trinity three years after San Jacinto. Lige recognized only two of the others: Jeff, the oldest of the Bailey boys, and Lee Hart, a Bailey wrangler.

"We got trouble," Mr. Bailey announced when Uncle Henry appeared. "Last night a handful o' Comanche boys run off a dozen o' my best horses. Set fire to the corncrib, too."

"Are you sure they were Comanches?" Uncle Henry asked. "There's been trouble with Yankee sympathizers up to Gainesville."

"Never saw a Yank run around with a painted chest, wavin' a lance an' screamin' to high heaven," Mr. Bailey told them. "I know an Indian when I see one. I lost three good men to 'em out on the Clear Fork o' the Brazos in '42."

"How do you know they were Comanches?" George asked. "No one's seen them out this way in over a year."

"Seein's one thing. Knowin' they were here's another. As to whether they were Comanche or some other tribe, I don't see it makes much difference. They stole my horses, and I aim to get after 'em."

"You'll never catch a small band like that, Nathan," Uncle Henry said. "Why don't you come inside, let Sally fix you something? We'll talk it out."

"Got no time for talk," Mr. Bailey said, turning his horse toward the river. "As for you, I'd post myself a good guard down in my horse pasture. An' I'd take it as a kindness if you'd look in on my Alice and the boys."

"You know I will," Uncle Henry said. "Good luck."

"Likely we'll need it," Mr. Bailey said, motioning for the other men to follow. "All of us."

Lige noticed a change in his uncle after that. There were a few extra wrinkles in Uncle Henry's forehead and a lot less laughter from everyone. The biggest difference to Lige was that he spent that night with George taking turns sleeping and keeping watch down in the pasture.

Occasionally Lige would spot a flicker of light from some spot up or down the river.

"Andrews aren't the only ones keeping watch," George told him. "Half the county's up keepin' an eye out for Comanches."

Lige nodded as he prepared to take over.

"Best thing to do is carry my musket in your arms, hugged close to you. Walk along the ridge, keepin' an eye on the river. Indians would most likely come in that way. If the steers get anxious, sing a little to 'em."

"Sing?"

"Lige, I've heard your singin'. It'll sound just like an old mama cow talkin' to her youngsters."

Lige laughed along with George, then set out to make his circle around the cattle. They'd rounded up all the horses and put them in the corral beside the barn. According to Uncle Henry, they'd be safe there.

"Comanches don't usually take to hittin' ranch houses and settlements. They like to hit quick and head for the hills."

That gave little comfort to Lige, who found himself jumping every time a lizard raced through the buffalo grass. He hummed and sang, not so much to soothe the cattle as to keep his mind off the darkness all around him.

> Oh, if I had myself a fine felt hat,
> I'd look as good as that dandy Matt.
> An' Susie'd ride in a carriage with me
> Down Jackson Street for all to see.

It was one of those stupid songs Brad had taught him when they were off stalking deer fall before last. There must have been a dozen others, all half-forgotten. Each of them came back to Lige that night as he kept watch. He was in the middle of a rather bawdy New Orleans lullaby when something moved through the high grass fifty yards or so to his left.

That's no lizard, Lige thought as he pulled back the

hammer of George's musket and swung the long barrel of the gun around to face the expected intruder.

"Hold on there," a deep voice called to him. "It's Zeke Jackson."

Lige lowered the barrel and eased the hammer back to its normal position. He felt his heart racing. His hands were moist, and it was all he could manage to catch his breath.

"Just came up to see if you had yourselves any coffee," Zeke explained as he emerged from the trees.

"I haven't seen any coffee in better'n a year," Lige said. "George has some o' that awful chicory mud brewin' on our fire, though. Want some?"

"That chicory coffee your Aunt Sally makes is the finest this side o' New Orleans, Lige," Zeke told him.

"Well, this is somethin' George boiled before goin' to sleep," Lige explained. "I wouldn't say for sure, but I think George might've added a bit o' shoe leather."

"Could be," Zeke said, laughing. "That George, he sure isn't much on cookin'."

Lige smiled and led the way to the fire. As they poured cups of the thick, muddy liquid, Zeke glanced around.

"Seems quiet enough," Lige whispered. "See anythin'?"

"Not likely to. Even if a Comanche was to come here, you'd not likely catch a glimpse of him. Might hear somethin'. Even then, you'd not know it was him. Indians can make themselves into all manner o' beasts—wolves, owls, even snakes."

"They can't either."

"Take my word for it, Lige. You think you hear some old wolf howlin' at the moon. But really it's a Comanche plannin' his steak dinner off your cows."

"He only sounds like a wolf, though."

"More'n that. To him, he is that wolf. He thinks wolf, smells wolf, is wolf. He may use a knife instead of teeth, but he'll strike just as hard an' run twice as fast."

"You know a lot about Indians."

"I spent some time with 'em. That was in my younger days," Zeke explained as he drank the coffee.

"When you were running away from the plantation?"

"No, after that. Doc Sam gave me my papers, an' I hadn't met up with Mary. So I used to work for the Quakers up to Fort Belknap. They'd need things taken down to the Kiowas, an' I'd hitch up my wagon an' deliver 'em. I got to where I could trade store-bought goods for hides, then sell the hides to the soldiers. I made a livin' for a time. Didn't last, though. The governor decided he wanted the Kiowas, Caddos, all of 'em, north o' the Red River. So the cavalry took 'em over."

"I remember. Papa took the soldiers some horses. I was there."

"That was one sad time, Lige Andrews."

"Why? I heard the Kiowas signed a treaty to go north."

"Not much choice to that. Go or stay and get killed. Those Kiowas, Lige, they'd taken to farmin', buildin' cabins even. Not to mention the Caddos an' Tonkawas. They tried to do things the white man's way, but it wasn't any good."

"How come?"

"'Cause the white men made themselves a broad avenue, but for a Kiowa or a black man it's a mighty narrow path. Not much room for wanderin', and a Kiowa's a natural born wanderer."

"And you?"

"Wanderer, wayfarer. One thing's certain. I'll never be nailed down to a farm like your papa or uncle, Lige. Isn't my way."

"Papa goes after horses in the rough country. We do a lot o' huntin'."

"That's not the same. Your papa'd rather spend the night in his rope bed, under a cotton quilt with a candle burnin' in the parlor. Me, this is my kind o' night, alone under the stars."

"Don't you miss your family?"

"I'd have 'em with me. Mary, now, she does take to quilts an' the like her own self, but Joe'd as soon race his pony through the mud as eat fried catfish."

"I'm like that, too."

"Then you've got a rocky trail ahead o' yourself, Lige. It's nigh impossible for a farm boy to wander. Not an' find himself any happiness."

Lige nodded. He'd already discovered that.

# 4

After that first night Lige and George took turns keeping watch over the cattle. Twice Lige sat alone on the hillside above the herd, humming softly and fighting the temptation to doze off. He kept the fire built high and bright, and George's rifle loaded and ready. But not so much as a shadow of an Indian disturbed the silence of the summer night.

As Lige saddled Skeeter once again for the ride to the pasture, Charlie joined him.

"How 'bout takin' me along tonight, Lige?" Charlie asked as Lige checked the cinch. "I could help guard."

"You'd be a lot of help," Lige said, lifting his brother up

and setting him on the fence. "You couldn't lift George's rifle, much less fire it."

"I could help you sing to the cows."

"That'd surely start a stampede. Two Andrews boys singin' the same night? That'd be worse'n a thunderstorm."

"I could keep you company."

"I'll be all right."

Charlie frowned and jumped down from the fence. He took off his straw hat and scratched his head.

"It's just that blamed owl, Lige," Charlie said, pointing to the loft.

"What owl?"

"The one that flies in the loft every night you're gone. He scares me half to death."

"Just lookin' for rats, most likely. And probably findin' one, too," Lige said, reaching under Charlie's arms and tickling the boy.

"I don't like owls. 'Sides, Brad says they're bad luck."

"Indian superstition. You'll be fine. Maybe Aunt Sally'll let you sleep in George's room."

"George snores."

"Well, you can't come with me. You'll be up all night, and I'll end up doin' your chores."

"I'll go to sleep."

"No," Lige said, pulling Charlie's hat down so that it covered the small boy's entire face.

"Lige?" Carol called out then.

Uncle Henry and Aunt Sally approached with George and Carol. George handed Lige the rifle, and Carol gave him a sack of paper cartridges and percussion caps.

"Thanks," Lige said, mounting his horse and resting the

rifle across one knee. He stuffed the cartridges in his trousers pocket.

"You watch out for yourself, Lige," Aunt Sally told him as she handed him a sack of dried beef bits and cold biscuits, along with some sassafras leaves for making tea.

"You remember now," Uncle Henry said, patting Lige's leg lightly. "You hear anything, even an owl call, fire off that rifle. George an' I'll be up in no time."

"Yes, sir," Lige said. It was the same thing his uncle had said each time. Still, it was a comforting thought to know help was so close at hand.

Lige gave them a farewell wave, then nudged Skeeter into a slow gallop. Soon Lige raced along with the wind in his face, his shaggy brown hair flying behind him as he wove his way toward the Trinity. As he crossed the narrow road leading north, he met up with Zeke Jackson.

"Kind of late in the day for travelin', isn't it?" Lige said, drawing up beside Zeke's wagon.

"I got to be at the Hayes place by mornin', Lige. I'll make it easy if I can get these farm boys off my road."

"Your road? This is my Uncle Henry's land."

"But my road. After all," Zeke said, smiling, "I'm the one who uses it. How can a road belong to a man who never goes anywhere?"

Lige pondered a minute, then shook his head.

"Does that mean if I had a horse I didn't ride, he wouldn't belong to me?"

"Well, I'll leave you to figure it out. I got work waitin' for me."

"What about the Comanches? Aren't you afraid to go at night?"

"What would they want with me? No, these'd likely be boys out provin' themselves, stealin' a few ponies, maybe a cow or two. I don't figure they want much of a battle."

"Aren't you worried about your family?"

"Joe's a fair shot. Mary's used to bein' left to herself. An' I don't figure you to let anything happen round here, Lige."

Lige frowned a bit as he saw Zeke was laughing.

"You watch yourself, Lige Andrews," Zeke said, stirring his horses into motion.

"You, too, Zeke," Lige said.

A few minutes later Lige reached the hillside and slid down from Skeeter's back. He tied the mustang to a small oak tree and left the animal to graze on the soft grasses there. He then began rounding up wood for his fire.

He spread out his blankets beside three large boulders. Then he poured some water into the coffeepot George had left from the night before. As he waited for the water to boil, he hummed softly to himself another of Brad's old tunes.

Suddenly there was the sound of someone moving in the tall grass behind him, and Lige jumped to his feet and swung the rifle around in that direction.

"Don't shoot!" Charlie cried out, stepping into the fading daylight. "It's only me!"

"Lord, Charlie, I could've shot you!" Lige screamed. "That'd be just fine. Papa asked me to look after you, and I put a lead ball in your fool brain."

"I'm sorry, Lige, but that owl's back."

"Why didn't you go and bother George?"

"He just ties me to the fence till I promise to go back up to the loft."

"I guess I ought to do that, too."

"Please, Lige, don't send me back. I can help."

"Do what? Fight Comanches?"

"There aren't really any Indians out here, are there?"

"Sure, and they love to scalp little boys with blond hair."

"You sure?"

"Zeke Jackson told me so."

"I guess it's true then. George says Zeke Jackson knows all about Indians."

"You ready to go back now?"

"I don't think I can find my way in the dark."

Lige frowned. It was getting darker, and he couldn't very well leave the cattle unattended while he took Charlie back to the house.

"You can stay if you promise to do just what I say," Lige said. "But don't you ever try this again, or I'll cut myself a switch and swing it till your backside's raw as a peeled onion."

Charlie sat down on the edge of Lige's blankets, and Lige added the sassafras to the boiling water. Soon they were sipping tea from tin cups.

In truth, it was nice to have some company, even if it was only Charlie. The nights had been getting longer, and Lige'd had about all of it he could take. Between the sound and the smell of the cattle, he was beginning to envy the corn farmers.

Except for some birds flittering around down by the river, the night was deathly quiet. Patches of clouds had swallowed the moon and half the stars. From time to time a covey of bobwhites would move about down the hill, and an occasional cricket would sound off.

Each noise magnified itself a thousand times in Lige's

ears. Every movement seemed to contain some Comanche warrior determined to get even with the hated white man by striking down poor Lige Andrews. Lige would usually walk out to see what the noise was, then return to the fire, and bite off a bit of dried beef or chew a biscuit.

"Scared?" Charlie asked.

"Sometimes," Lige admitted. "Not so much of the Indians, but of what I can't see."

"Maybe there's ghosts around. Remember the story Seth told us about that man who got himself hung out here?"

"Just a story. Why don't you go to sleep?"

"I'll try," Charlie said, curling up into a horseshoe beside the fire.

On past midnight Lige was half sleeping when he heard a twig snap fifty feet or so away. The cattle began moving around restlessly, and he shook himself awake.

"What was that?" Charlie whispered as a similar sound once again shattered the stillness of the night.

"I guess I'd best take a look. Stay here."

"Lige?" Charlie said, wrapping one arm around Lige's legs and holding him in place.

"I have to go see what it is, Charlie," Lige explained. Just stay right here. It's likely nothin' at all."

But as Lige drew back the hammer of George's musket and set off into the thick underbrush, another sound and another attracted his attention. Whatever it was appeared to be circling around to the southwest. Lige followed cautiously.

It was too dark to see anything clearly, but Lige's instincts told him someone was moving around in the trees below. The cattle were growing nervous, and Skeeter broke loose from the tree and trotted down to where Lige was standing.

They know what they're doing, Lige thought as he continued to stalk the intruders. Coming at night, when only Lige was there to guard the cattle. He could fire the rifle and alert Uncle Henry and George, not to mention the other farmers and ranchers along the river. But it would take precious minutes to reload the rifle, and he'd be defenseless in the meantime.

What do I do? Lige asked himself. There was no easy answer. Suddenly he heard three loud whoops from across the river. A horse splashed into the water. Then there was an outbreak of flame from the prairie beyond.

Zeke's cabin, Lige thought. I hope Joe got his mama and brother and sister away.

A single shot exploded close by, and Lige felt himself die a little inside. That could only mean the Indians or whoever it was had caught the Jacksons in the open. But he had little time to think about that. Just below him a single Comanche rose to his feet, shook something at Lige, and vanished. For a second Lige was confused. Then he heard a high-pitched cry. He understood.

He'd been decoyed. Lige turned and raced back toward the fire.

"Charlie, run!" Lige screamed.

When he reached the fire, the blankets lay there as before, but there was no sign of Lige's brother.

"Oh, Lord, not Charlie," Lige cried, looking in every direction at once. He spotted footprints in the ground to his right and crept forward, studying the ground carefully. Twenty feet or so down the trail he discovered Charlie's hat.

45

Continuing, he reached a clearing. At the far end several Indians were skinning a steer. On the left a few others seemed to be putting something onto the back of a horse. Lige bit his lip as he caught a glimpse of blond hair.

It was Charlie. But what could Lige do? There were half a dozen Indians down there. What hope was there of rescuing his brother?

The cattle stirred about restlessly, and Lige had an idea. He turned the rifle in their direction and fired it. The concussion shook the leaves all around him and sent the cattle stampeding toward the river.

The Comanches screamed and took off on horseback after the animals. But a rampaging herd of cattle could rarely be headed off. While the Indians were occupied with the cattle, Lige crept closer to Charlie. But when he came to within fifty feet, a tall bare-chested warrior stepped out toward him with a raised lance.

Lige froze. He fumbled with the ramrod and tried to find one of the paper cartridges Carol had handed him. He tore it open and poured the powder down the barrel. Then he rammed the ball home and slipped a fresh cap beneath the hammer. He cocked the rifle and prepared to fire. But his fingers were unable to move.

The Comanche hurled the lance into the ground in front of Lige and taunted him to come forward. Lige slipped around behind a tall oak. It seemed impossible the Indian could know he was there. Still the Comanche gestured wildly.

He knows I won't, Lige thought. He knows I don't want to die, not even to save my little brother. He knows I'm a coward.

The words cut through him like a knife, chilling him, bringing a throbbing sensation to his head. Still Lige remained there, frozen, powerless. Finally the Comanche spit on the ground and turned. Moments later the Indians were riding away into the night, carrying with them a few slaughtered beefs and one small boy.

# 5

Lige was standing beside the oak in the dim moonlight when George arrived. Lige's eyes were glazed, and he said nothing as George took the rifle from his hands and set it beside the tree.

"Lige?" George asked.

"They came," Lige said, leading the way down the hill to the slaughtered steer.

"I know," George said, helping Lige to the river. They sat together, staring at the bright orange flames dancing from the ruin of Zeke Jackson's cabin across the river and from the Bailey barn downstream. The entire county was awake. Settlers rode by with rifles, searching for the raiders.

"They took Charlie," Lige mumbled, looking off into the hills to the north.

"How?"

"He followed me out here. He was scared of an owl."

Lige dropped his face into his hands. A picture appeared in his mind, of Charlie—splashing through the shallows of the river, laughing as he fell out of a tree or chased a pig through the mud. Next he saw Charlie, bound from head to toe, riding crosswise on a spotted pony, headed for the uncertainties of life as a Comanche captive.

"We'll find him," George said, resting a hand on Lige's shoulder. "Come on back home."

Lige didn't remember much of what followed. He lay in George's bed half the day, drifting in and out of a nightmare-haunted slumber. Carol brought him dinner—slices of beef and some fried potatoes and greens from Aunt Sally's garden.

"I just stood there," Lige said, remembering the Comanche's taunts. "I let 'em take him."

"There wasn't anything you could do, Lige. They hit the Bailey house, took Mrs. Bailey and little Ellen. Travis, too."

"They burned Zeke's house."

"More than that, Lige," Carol said, squeezing his hand. "Nobody knows for sure what happened, but when Papa and George rode over there this morning, they found Joe shot outside the cabin."

Lige gripped her fingers tightly as she continued.

"They had Tyler Ramsey, too, but he slipped away last night. He stumbled home this afternoon."

"Did he see Charlie?"

"Yes. And the Baileys."

"What about the Jacksons?"

"Mary and Lizzie were all right. James, though . . . "

"What?"

"They had him walking along. He couldn't keep up, so they . . . "

"Killed him?"

"Yes."

Lige closed his eyes and released Carol's hand. Another nightmare appeared in his mind—a Comanche dragging Charlie along, screaming at the little boy to keep up. Then the Indian drew out a knife and . . .

"Lige, he'll be fine. George and Papa rode off to look for him," Carol whispered.

"I ought to've gone, too. It's my fault."

"You couldn't fight twenty Comanches."

"Joe tried."

"He's dead, too."

"I should've done something," Lige said, shivering. "All I did was hide."

George and Uncle Henry returned at dusk. With them were Mr. Bailey and the men who'd left the week before.

"We found a trail," George explained to Lige that night, "but we lost it. We'll try again later."

But Lige knew from the look in George's eyes that there wasn't much hope. Charlie was gone.

The next morning Lige got up and tended to his chores. He hoped the work would keep his mind off Charlie, but it didn't. Uncle Henry had them move the cattle away from the river, back to a small meadow between two ponds.

There were other things to be done as well. The Jackson boys were buried beneath three tall willow trees atop Boulder Hill. The Bailey barn was rebuilt, and patrols by the militia were kept up along the Trinity.

No one went anywhere unarmed or alone. And there was a cloud of fear over the entire countryside.

It was a week later that Zeke Jackson rode to the Andrews' ranch. He eased his horse forward until he was directly in front of Lige.

No one who saw Zeke sit a horse would ever forget the sight. He wore a vest of buffalo hide over a rough buckskin shirt and trousers, and his great dark eyes peered out from under a broad-brimmed cowhide hat. A long Sharp's rifle rested in a scabbard beside his saddle, and a Colt revolver protruded from his belt.

There was something unearthly about the man. Deep wrinkles were etched in his forehead, and he moved a little like a shadow in the late afternoon sunlight.

"Where's Mary?" Zeke asked in a loud voice. "Where're my boys an' Lizzie?"

Lige looked around for someone else to answer, but the words seemed to be seeking him out, flying through the air like Comanche arrows aimed at his heart.

"Lige Andrews, you seen Joe and James?" Zeke asked. "What's come of my Mary?"

"The Comanches were here," Lige mumbled, trying to avoid the man's probing eyes.

"Any fool could see that. My cabin's burned. My barn's down. There's Comanche and Kiowa sign everywhere. Now you tell me, Lige, where's my family?"

"I was down by the river watchin' Uncle Henry's

cows," Lige said, trying to keep from trembling. "The Indians came. They took Charlie. And all I did was watch."

Zeke scowled. He moved a little closer, then climbed down from his horse and leaned on the fence post next to Lige.

"They were at your cabin, too," Lige explained. "I saw some smoke. I guess Joe tried to fight. He didn't have much of a chance. They killed him. James, too. I should've helped. But all I did was hide."

Lige hung his head and started to walk away, but Zeke reached out and held him in place.

"Mary, too?" Zeke asked. "An' Lizzie?"

"No. The Comanches took 'em both. Charlie, too. Ty Ramsey saw 'em. He got away. I guess the Indians took 'em up north into the Nations."

"Would seem likely," Zeke said, sitting on a nearby rock.

"I'm sorry," Lige said, shaking. "I should've gone down there, helped Joe, got help."

"Just got yourself killed's all," Zeke said, sadness filling his great brown eyes. "No, nobody could've stopped it. 'Cept me maybe."

"You?"

"Mary always said I was gone too much. It's a trial for a good woman to take herself a wanderin' man. Where'd they put my boys, Lige? Where are Joe and James?"

"Up on Boulder Hill, just above the creek. It's nice up there."

"Flowers every spring. That's good. Shade trees, too."

"Want me to take you there? It's not far."

"No, I believe I'll go up there myself in a bit. I want

to find some stones, make markers. A father ought to do that for his boys, don't you think? Ought to do that at least."

Lige expected Zeke to cry, but no tears came. No, he won't do it in front of me, Lige told himself. He'll save it for Boulder Hill, for Joe and James.

"I could help with the markers," Lige offered. "Maybe pick some wildflowers down by the river."

"Don't trouble yourself," Zeke said, getting to his feet. "I'll attend to it."

"We were fishin' together just the other day."

"They're in good hands now, Lige," Zeke told him. "You look after yourself."

Lige nodded as Zeke mounted his horse.

"Tell your uncle I'd like to speak with him later on," Zeke said.

"I will."

Zeke turned toward the creek and eased his horse into a trot. Lige put aside his work and walked to the house to pass on Zeke's message.

The following morning Zeke met with Mr. Bailey and Uncle Henry. Lige looked on nervously as Mr. Bailey listened. There'd never been many dealings between Zeke and the Baileys. Except for shoeing the horses twice a year, Lige didn't suppose Zeke had been on Bailey land.

"I heard you rode after the Comanches," Zeke said, not bothering to dismount. "Twice."

"They took my wife, one of my boys an' my little girl. I'll go again when I've rounded up enough help," Mr. Bailey said.

"Little point to that," Zeke said. "The country's hard up there, and the Comanches'll be scattered."

"They've got my family!"

"An' my Mary an' Lizzie. You never had much use for my words before, but you listen good to 'em now. I know the Comanche, the Kiowa. I've treated with 'em. When I was a little more'n Lige's age, I hauled flour to the Kiowas at Belknap. Twice a month I'd ride down to the lodges, swappin' for hides an' such. I'll go myself. Find me good horses, corn liquor, and iron hatchets, good rifles. These'll get your wife, the little ones back."

"I'll be ridin' with you," Mr. Bailey said.

"And me," Uncle Henry added.

"I ride alone. I got a chance to bring them back," Zeke said solemnly. "Comanches got no love of white men. You go, we'll all bleach in the sun by summer's end."

"There's got to be another way. You can scout for us," Mr. Bailey suggested.

"No," Zeke said, shaking his head.

"But we've got to do something," Uncle Henry said.

"You will be," Zeke told them.

"Then it's settled," Mr. Bailey said. "You'll leave as soon as we raise the trade goods. You'll deal with the Indians."

Zeke nodded, then turned his horse and rode away.

Lige and George took the trade goods to the scarred rubble of Zeke's cabin at dawn the next day. Nothing much was said as the goods were packed on the horses and in the wagon. Afterward George started back home, but Lige lingered.

"Did you get the markers finished?" Lige asked.

Zeke nodded and went on checking the ropes on the pack horses.

"It's good to put up reminders," Lige said, picking up the singed remains of a rag doll. "People shouldn't be forgotten."

"Forgotten?" Zeke asked, looking up from his work. "A man doesn't forget his family, the little boys he held in his hands. Oh, Lord, I miss 'em. I expect Lizzie to come runnin' in from the fields, to catch Joe an' James sneakin' pieces of their mama's pies. An' Mary . . . Oh, Lord, look after 'em all."

Lige glanced at his feet, then stared off into the distance a moment. "I never thought much about it, but I miss Charlie. He used to annoy me, always gettin' in the way and such. But he's my brother."

"I'll do my best to bring him home, Lige."

Lige set down the doll and walked over to where a Comanche lance lay embedded in a locust tree. Lige worked the point loose, then smashed the shaft against the tree.

"I hate 'em!" Lige screamed. "I wish I could kill 'em, every one of 'em."

Zeke turned and took the splintered lance from Lige's hand.

"They're murderers," Lige said bitterly. "And they took my little brother. I hate 'em."

"Sit down right here a minute, Lige Andrews!" Zeke hollered, forcing Lige to the ground with a heavy hand. "Don't you think other people round here got cause to hurt? You figure you're the only one to feel anything?"

Lige stared hard into Zeke's fiery brown eyes.

"My boys're buried up there!" Zeke yelled, swinging his arm out toward Boulder Hill. "My Mary's off with 'em. My little girl. But that don't make Comanches better nor worse'n they were before. They live by a code, just like you do. This was their place 'fore it was yours, an' all they're doin' is hittin' back the only way they know how."

"I never did anything to them. Neither did Charlie."

"You got this all twisted in your head, Lige, if you think it's got anythin' at all to do with you or Charlie or my Mary. It's a war that's been ragin' here for years. Comanches can't ride down here, chase us all off this land. So they raid, kill a few, run off some stock. And the army used to go up north an' punish 'em. Only now there's no army, so the Indians get a bit more venturesome."

"We never went into their towns an' killed their families."

"It's been done, Lige. An' then there's the sickness."

"Sickness?"

"All sorts o' fevers. One winter I watched the Kiowas die off from a pox. We stacked bodies like cordwood."

"So what're you sayin'? That I'm not supposed to hate 'em?"

"I'm not your daddy, Lige. It's not my place to tell you a thing."

"I wish somebody would."

"It's time you did your own decidin' about things. I'm no one to judge for anybody else. But hate, Lige, it eats a man up. I used to hate white men. I hated 'em for puttin' chains on me, for beatin' my mama and sellin' my daddy off to some planter downstate to Columbia. But then 'long comes Dr. Sam, an' he gives us all our freedom papers. Now that causes a man to think. Don't hate when somethin' happens to you. Figure out what you can do 'bout it, an' do it."

"But there's nothin' I can do."

Zeke looked off into the distance. "I know what that feels like, Lige. I surely do."

That night Lige sat alone in the loft, wiping the sweat from his forehead and thinking about what Zeke had said. Do something. But what was there Lige could do?

Nothing.

He turned to the empty blankets to his right. Charlie should be there, squirming around in the straw, whistling some tired old tune or asking a thousand questions. Lige could almost see the unkempt head of blond hair, the small feet resting in a pile of hay.

Lige closed his eyes and tried to forget. But an image of his brother appeared. There was Charlie, enduring a hundred tortures, a thousand hardships. And Lige felt each and every one.

Lige glanced out the loft window. Off in the distant hills a fire was burning. That would be Zeke, making camp at the end of the first day's journey. There'd be many such nights and countless miles ahead of him.

"I wish they'd taken me instead," Lige said, touching the blankets that should have been covering his brother. "I do, Charlie."

Lige looked back at the tiny prick of light coming from the far horizon. It could get cold out there at night, all alone with no end in sight for your journey. But he was cold right there, in the barn, even though the place was sweltering. As he thought about Charlie, frigid, icy fingers seemed to run through his insides, chilling every inch of his being.

It was hard to say what prompted him to pull on his trousers and climb down the ladder to the barn, why he threw a saddle onto Skeeter's back. Certainly no one with any sense rode off alone at night into the far hills.

It won't be easy finding Zeke in the darkness, Lige told himself. And Zeke said he rode alone. But Lige knew all about loneliness. He'd known nothing else from the instant the Comanches had carried away his brother.

"I'm going to bring you home, Charlie," Lige whispered.

He was like a shadow as he made his way through the house, taking Grandpa Clark's old Colt pistol from its hiding place in George's room, filling a deerskin bag with jerked beef and corn cakes. After leaving a short note for his aunt and uncle, Lige walked to the barn and collected a steel hunting knife and enough percussion caps and balls to keep his pistol armed throughout the trip.

He then crept quietly to the corral and led Skeeter out the gate. He mounted the horse at the edge of the cornfield and nudged it into a slow trot. Soon he'd be sharing that fire with Zeke Jackson. And before long he'd see Charlie again. The thought warmed him all over.

Lige rode briskly down the old trail toward the hills, weaving his way through the oaks and locusts. He possessed a new energy, greater confidence. He felt taller in the saddle than he'd ever felt before.

# 6

The night seemed to grow darker as Lige continued riding. Occasionally the yellow flicker of Zeke's campfire would fade and even disappear. Lige would blink his eyes and pray the light would appear once more.

The going was slow and tedious. Gullies lurked just beyond the edge of the trail, eager to swallow any unsuspecting traveler. The eerie calls of owls echoed through the stillness, and every few minutes Lige froze as the midnight shadow of a locust limb or the darting figure of a deer surprised him. Memories of the Comanches were never far from his thoughts, and twice he cocked the huge Colt revolver and prepared to deal death to his enemies.

As he rode onward, Lige found his eyelids growing

heavier by the moment. He tried to blink away the weariness, but he had little success.

His eyes closed, and he was only partially aware of the world around him. Skeeter moved along, sensing the correct path, stepping lively on the downhill stretches, plodding along faithfully as the road turned uphill.

The only thing that kept Lige going was the dream of Charlie being chased around a Comanche camp by a fearsome warrior. Lige saw it every time he drifted toward sleep. A terrible cloud of guilt would descend on him, and he'd cough away the exhaustion and urge Skeeter into a trot.

He didn't know for sure when it was that he approached the camp. Long before he saw the horses, he smelled the smoke from Zeke's cooking fire. Sausage, Lige guessed. And something else. Red peppers maybe. It aroused a rumbling in Lige's stomach.

Lige pulled on the reins, and Skeeter drew to a halt. He slid down from the saddle, then cautiously led the horse forward. Smoke lay heavy in the air, partially obscuring a clearing and a small pond.

Suddenly Lige heard a musket's hammer clicking into place. He released Skeeter's reins and sat perfectly still.

"Hold on there," a voice boomed out from behind him. "I don't recall invitin' any strangers into my camp."

Lige trembled a second. Then he made a slow turn around, keeping his hands out to each side, in as plain a view as possible in the dim light.

"It's me, Zeke," Lige announced. "Lige Andrews."

"What you doin' up here, boy?" Zeke said, stepping out of the shadows. "No time for boys to be ridin' about."

"I followed you."

"Well, I heard o' brighter things than that bein' done. What you want to follow me for?"

"I want to come along."

"Well, you won't be doin' any such thing as that, Lige Andrews, and that's the Lord's own truth. Comin' along! My, I always thought you were the smart one in your daddy's family, too. Comin' along! Like to get us both scalped! I don't plan givin' up no hair o' mine this year or next."

Zeke walked up beside Lige and reached out his big black hands. Lige felt his knees wobble, but Zeke took him by the shoulders and frowned.

"What you got here?" Zeke asked, glancing down at the pistol in Lige's belt.

"This?" Lige asked, pulling the gun from his belt and showing it off. "Grandpa left it to me. It's a Colt dragoon pistol."

"I know the piece," Zeke said, releasing Lige and taking the revolver in his hands. The man turned the gun over and over, smiling faintly. "Cap'n Handley back at Belknap had one o' these. I once watched him shave a branch off a cedar at fifty feet. That was out past the Brazos, as I remember it. Too much gun for a boy to be foolin' with."

"I can shoot it. I hit a turkey last October."

"Didn't leave much to eat, did it?"

"No," Lige said, shaking his head.

Zeke returned the gun and turned away. Lige stuffed the pistol in his belt, took Skeeter's reins in his left hand and followed as Zeke led the way to the cooking fire.

"You can tie your horse over there," Zeke said, pointing to a scrub oak near the pond. The other animals stood

61

nearby. "Bed down where you like. Tomorrow you'll be goin' home."

"I'm going across the Red River with you," Lige said.

"You'll be doin' many things in your life, Lige Andrews, but that won't be one of 'em. That you can be blamed sure of. I won't be packin' no kids into Comanche lands, no siree. In particular, I won't be packin' no white ones. There's too many better ways for a man to get himself scalped."

Lige wanted to argue, but he was too tired. Morning was almost upon them. He unsaddled Skeeter and tied the reins to a low limb. Then Lige threw his blankets on the hard cold ground and sat down. He got out of his boots, pulled off his trousers, and squirmed between the scratchy wool of the blankets. Before he knew it, he was lost to the world.

But it proved to be a less than peaceful sleep. Even as morning sunlight was flooding the camp, Lige was tossing and turning, flaying his arms, and shouting at the sky.

"No! No! No!" he screamed. "Let him be! Charlie, run!"

Lige found himself back at the river, surrounded by a hundred Comanches, all taunting him with their lances and grinning as they held knives to Charlie's throat.

"Let him be! Take me instead!"

But the Indians just laughed. Then they threw Charlie on a horse and rode away, leaving Lige standing there alone, helpless.

"Lige, you best wake up," Zeke said, shaking Lige's shoulder. "You're just havin' yourself a nightmare's all. Best wake up now. I got to be leavin', and you got to be headin' back."

Lige sat up and rubbed the sleep out of his eyes. He was

shaking like a leaf in an October wind, barely hanging on, struggling to make some sense out of what was going on.

"You all right, boy?"

"Yeah," Lige said, shaking away the dream. Even so it lingered. Phantom Comanches emerged from the shadows of oak trees. Charlie's frightened face grew out of the sun.

"You had yourself a long night, Lige," Zeke told him. "You'll be feelin' better when you get back home."

"I'm not going back," Lige said, rolling up his blankets. "I'm going on with you."

"Oh, no. You won't be doin' any such fool thing."

"I'm near as good a tracker as there is around, Zeke. I can smell a man half a mile away. I can ride all day. I'm not bad company, and I can spell you on night watch or leadin' the horses."

"That'd be fine if we was headin' for the Overland way station down on the Brazos. But we're headin' for Comanches, an' all the use they got for white boys, Lige, is slittin' them for amusement."

"They got Charlie, Zeke."

"An' others, too. I aim to bring 'em all back, Lige. Can't do that if I'm dead."

"I promise, Zeke. I won't get in the way. An' if it does come to fightin', I can be some help."

"Look, boy, I know it rests heavy with you those Comanches got little Charlie, but that's not goin' to change by you goin' north. Comanches won't treat with me if they see I got a white boy along. They trust me a little as a black man. I traded with 'em before. But they never deal with whites, not lately. They'd kill you 'fore you could say 'good mornin'.'"

"I've got to go, Zeke. You can take out ahead of me, but I'll just follow. You can't hide these horses like one of Mama's thimbles."

"You goin' to get us killed, Lige Andrews. Then that little brother o' yours won't be comin' back."

Lige swallowed the words he was about to speak and glanced around. Zeke had a small fire going. A smoke-blackened pot lay at one end. A slab of bacon stood ready for cooking, and four fresh eggs rested in a basin.

"Hungry?" Zeke asked, seeming to read Lige's mind.

"Starved," Lige said.

Soon they were sharing a hearty breakfast. The food revived Lige's spirits, and he prepared to renew the argument. When Zeke began packing the horses for the day's ride, Lige pitched in.

"I've got to go with you," Lige said softly.

"No," Zeke answered him firmly.

"I've made up my mind," Lige said.

"Look, you best get somethin' understood!" Zeke shouted, turning around and facing Lige with a look that threatened violence. "You ain't the one doin' the decidin', not here, not now, not ever! I got somethin' to do. I got six people up there in some Comanche camp waitin' for a chance to get back home. You can't keep me from doin' that, boy. Isn't to be."

Lige stared at the ground and sighed. "You're probably right. I'd get in the way, get you all killed."

Lige sat down. A great emptiness filled him. "It's my fault, you know," He finally said. "I could have stopped them. There was this Comanche. He stood there right in front of me, just waiting for me to step out and fight. He even threw his lance in the ground. I had George's rifle. All I had to do was aim and fire. But I couldn't."

"Shootin' at a man's never an easy thing to do," Zeke said, sitting next to Lige.

"I knew they were over at your place, too. If I'd fired my rifle, George an' Uncle Henry would've come. Maybe Joe would still be alive."

"Comanches likely killed him the moment they hit the place. An' it's certain they'd have killed you. No, you had your life to live, Lige. Could've been the other way round."

"An' what about Charlie? I was supposed to take care of him. I promised Papa before we left home."

"A man does the best he can, Lige. Can't blame himself after. Life's hard sometimes. Things happen you don't always understand. Lord makes it tough on some folk."

"Sure does," Lige said, sinking his chin into his hands.

"But the world turns round, they say. Even a snake swaps his old skin for a new one. Life has its turns, too."

"I suppose."

"I'll make a point to find him, Lige."

"It's not your job," Lige said, staring off past the pond. "It's my fault he's gone. It's my duty to bring him home."

A strange look came over Zeke's face. Then a sparkle came to his deep brown eyes.

"Ever got yourself burned bad in the sun, Lige?" Zeke asked.

"Not that I remember. I get tanned by late April."

"I seen white boys burn bright pink, just like the inside of a Mississippi peach. You know what Doc Sam does for 'em?"

"No," Lige said, only half paying attention.

"He puts a little berry juice on 'em. Stains their skin. Makes it sort o' dark brown."

"So?"

"Comanche brown, they call it."

"And?"

"Your hair's dark enough. Put a little berry juice on, walk round an' let the sun work on it, you might make a fair imitation o' Caddo, maybe Tonkawa."

"Maybe Comanches wouldn't scalp an Indian."

"An' maybe not a black man travelin' with a Tonkawa boy. Know any Indian words?"

"No," Lige said sadly.

"Spanish?"

"A few."

"Well, we'd best do a good bit o' practicin' 'tween now an' Red River Crossin'. Elsewise, only songs sung for us'll be by Comanche bucks talkin' 'bout their lodgepoles. An' the hair they got hangin' there."

Lige managed a faint smile.

"It's a fool thing to do, Lige. But nobody ever said Zeke Jackson had a lot o' sense."

They spent the whole day at Hunter's Pond, resting and readying themselves for the difficult days ahead. As they lay beside the dying embers of the cooking fire that night, Lige sighed. I won't just be playin' Indian this time, though, he told himself. I have to be Indian, speak Indian, act Indian. Otherwise, I'll get us both killed. But as he stared at the stars overhead, he found himself imagining the terror that had filled Charlie's eyes as the Comanches carried him off.

Won't be much longer now, Charlie, Lige thought. I'm on my way.

# 7

Lige slept better that night in the little camp beside Hunter's Pond, but not as long as he would have liked. Well before daybreak Zeke roused him, issuing commands like some kind of army general.

I might as well be back home, Lige thought as he collected wood for the breakfast fire. Chores and more chores.

Lige said nothing, though. He hadn't been invited, and like all unwelcome guests, he had no right to complain.

Once they hit the trail, it was little better. Zeke kept to himself as he led the way. Occasionally he'd hum to the pack horses, but rarely did he smile or speak.

Lige spent those incredibly long hours on the road riding Skeeter, leading two of the trade ponies and relying on

Zeke's knowledge of the trail to guide his own movements.

From time to time Lige would ride up alongside Zeke and ask questions. There was so much Lige hungered to know. Where would the Comanches locate their camps? Where might they keep captives? How would Zeke convince them to give up Charlie and the others? But Zeke only shook his head and went on humming.

"Time'd be better spent practicin' your Spanish words, Lige Andrews," Zeke finally said. "Even if we get you to look passable like a Tonkawa, you don't sound like one."

So Lige tried to call out the Spanish names for everything he saw—the birds, the trees, the hills and the streams. Often Zeke would correct the accent. Lige sometimes missed a word altogether, and Zeke would bellow with laughter. Lige once thought the man's eyes might come right out of their sockets.

"It wasn't that funny," Lige complained.

"Oh, no?" Zeke asked. "Why, you just said you'd paint a cactus and cook your tongue."

Lige tried to frown, but Zeke was shaking from head to toe. The laughter was contagious, and for the first time, the two companions shared something more than the July heat and a common trail.

But it didn't last. Before long Zeke had drifted away again. There was a strange, faraway look in those brown eyes. Lige knew that look, and he realized that Zeke was being haunted, too. And no matter what he might say, Lige told himself, Zeke can't help noticing I'm still alive while Joe and James aren't. Maybe he'll trade me to the Comanches for his family. Well, Lige thought, if Zeke gets Charlie back, it will be worth it.

"For once I won't have failed," Lige remarked as they threaded their way along the narrow road past Buffalo Springs. Lige had half a thought to turn Skeeter and ride up to the cluster of ramshackle buildings. But there wasn't a sign of life there. The usually busy cantina was deserted, and not a single trader appeared as Zeke led the way past the springs northward.

Lige knew the war had sent many of the hide hunters and traders who roamed the northwest frontier into the army. And he guessed the others had been persuaded by marauding bands of Kiowa and Comanche raiders that other country might be safer. Zeke never gave the place a second look.

They managed another twenty miles before darkness began closing in. Zeke halted in the center of a stand of black locusts—tall, stately trees that clustered around a natural spring. As Lige climbed off Skeeter, his nostrils filled with the scent of fresh water.

"A river," Lige cried out, rushing forward. "Water!"

Lige peeled off his dusty clothes and plunged into the shallow water. The icy liquid revived him. He shivered away his exhaustion and screamed out in delight.

Zeke sat on the bank with the long Sharp's rifle in his hands. It was only then Lige realized this wasn't home. He nervously waded to the shore, picked up his clothes, and rejoined Zeke.

"Guess that wasn't the smartest thing anybody ever did," Lige said.

"Well, anybody round knows we're here," Zeke said, shaking his head.

"Sorry."

"Every man's due one or two pieces o' pure ole luck, Lige. You just used up one. Don't press for the other too soon."

After eating a cold supper of beef bits and onions, Zeke led the way back to the river. They scrubbed their clothes, filled water casks, and dug for tubers.

"We're not still on the Trinity, are we?" Lige asked, taking a long drink from his canteen.

"West Fork," Zeke said, nodding his head. "Curls round. You can follow her just short o' the Little Wichita. Then it's up to Red River Crossin'."

"An' then into the Nations?"

"Unless we meet up with Comanches 'fore that. Mostly, though, it's too close to the settlements now for 'em. Maybe tomorrow, though, we'll be runnin' across some bands."

"What makes you think they won't kill us?"

"Don't know as they won't. But I traded with 'em once. It's easier to trade with a man for what you want than to shoot him. An' a whole lot safer. We might shoot back."

Lige laughed. But Zeke was in a somber mood. The man walked over to a boulder and sat down. He took out a knife and began whittling on a small block of wood.

"I've never been this far from home before," Lige said, sitting nearby. "Only to Buffalo Springs and old Fort Belknap. Papa promises to take me to market, only it's always next year."

"I took Joe to the crossing once," Zeke said. "He stood tall as a white oak for a week after that. We shot deer hereabouts."

"Joe was a good shot."

"Had a nose for game. Better'n a hound for scarin' up birds."

"Nobody could outswim him."

Zeke turned away, and Lige tossed a rock at a willow tree. Lige knew Zeke was crying inside. There must be something I can do to help, Lige told himself.

"I never got to know my own daddy," Zeke said, breaking the silence. "He got himself sold downriver when I was no older'n Lizzie. I wanted to give my boys more."

As Zeke talked about Joe and James, little smiles would come and go from the man's face. They'd shared so much. Lige felt his insides twist into knots as he thought about how it was with his own father, how tough it had always been to measure up.

"I guess a man can't face a greater sadness than to see his boys laid in the ground ahead of him," Zeke spoke softly.

Lige wondered if it would bother his father so much.

That night as they prepared their beds, Zeke made a thorough search of the nearby woods.

"Three more days to Red River Crossing," Zeke finally announced. "Lots of scavengers about. We'd best keep our eyes out tonight. Could be trouble."

Lige kept his pistol beside him that night and woke at every sound.

As it turned out, though, the night was uneventful. Except for a prowling skunk, no visitors had appeared in the locust grove when the sun brightened the eastern horizon. By then Zeke had a fire going, and Lige was busy getting the horses ready.

The Trinity crossing took better than an hour. Heavy rainfall in the country to the west made the normal ford unusable. They found a shallow spot three miles farther east. Lige and Zeke swam the animals to the far bank, then floated their supplies across.

They made their way slowly those next two days, cautiously traversing the low hills cut by the Little Wichita. Zeke slowed the pace with each succeeding mile, and Lige found himself searching the surrounding woods, half expecting a Comanche war party to emerge any second.

"We'll be at the crossin' tomorrow," Zeke said as Lige led the horses to a pool of water formed by a small rock spring. "If any of that Andrews luck's still with you, Lige, wish us a clear road."

Lige closed his eyes a minute and imagined them alone on the road. A hundred Comanches circled, howling and pointing at the two fools who were trying to hold off a whole war party.

"You go on and build us a fire tonight, Lige," Zeke said, pointing out a spot near a small cottonwood. "Be sure to use hardwood. Don't want smoke on the wind for twenty miles."

Lige nodded.

"I could use myself a little warm supper," Zeke said, pacing around the camp. "What's left of the food?"

Lige peeked inside the cloth food sack. There was almost nothing there.

"That bad, huh?" Zeke said, observing Lige's disappointment. "I hunted deer not far from here one time. I'll bet we could have a fine dinner, maybe venison steaks an' some o' those greens I saw down by the spring."

"Collards."

"I believe there's plums there, too, if the birds didn't already get 'em all."

"Seems late for plums."

"No, spring rains came in mid-May."

Lige didn't argue, but neither did he find any plums left to pick. Once firewood was collected, Zeke waved for Lige to follow.

"You bring a rifle?" Zeke asked.

"Just Grandpa's Colt," Lige said.

"You really fire that cannon?"

Lige nodded.

"Well, I wouldn't count on puttin' down a deer with it. Go take my old Enfield off o' my horse. There's caps an' powder. You know how to make cartridges?"

"I've made my share," Lige said, spitting. He didn't look forward to biting open the paper of the cartridges. They always tasted of sulphur and stung his eyes.

"Get along to it then," Zeke said.

Lige took the rifled musket and rested it on his left shoulder. He then marched back to Zeke soldier style, humming a military march Seth had taught him.

"Know how to load?" Zeke asked.

"I've done it."

"Then put one round down her gullet. Wait on the cap. Wouldn't want you shootin' your own poor partner with that thing."

Lige smiled. He'd nearly done just that a year earlier

when he'd gone out with Brad. It seemed much funnier now than it had then. Before Lige could do any more remembering, though, Zeke disappeared into a nearby thicket. Lige hurried to join him.

"I done this a few times with Joe and James," Zeke whispered. "James wasn't much of a shot, but his eyes were sharp as a hawk's. Joe, now, he was a hunter. He could track anything that had legs. Wasn't much for doin' chores round the farm, but he could hunt butterflies in a snowstorm."

Lige laughed. As they threaded their way through the thicket, Lige found himself recalling the many times he'd hunted with Brad or George. It brought a shudder through his weary shoulders, but he refused to give way to emotion. He walked on. Just ahead Zeke froze. A large doe was eating grass twenty yards or so away. Lige placed the percussion cap on his musket, cocked the piece, and awaited Zeke's direction. The moment that it was given, the two guns fired, and the deer fell dead.

"We got her!" Lige yelled.

"Yes. Now help me with the skinnin'."

It was an unpleasant job. Lige knew he should have offered to do all the work, what with Zeke providing a place to sleep and guiding them down the road. But Lige knew little about how to do it, and Zeke seemed willing to instruct.

"You've got a fair eye with that rifle," Zeke observed as they worked together. "You know the woods. I guess maybe you earned your spot today. But it'd likely be better if you stayed behind once we cross the Red River. It's dangerous at the crossin', and worse once we land in the Nations."

"I have to go on," Lige said, and there was no further debate.

What they didn't eat for dinner that night was smoked and dried. It would provide a food reserve for the long journey north into the unknown. As night began to fall, Lige stared at the stars and thought about Charlie.

Zeke looked above, too, and Lige could tell the man was remembering. A sadness filled the air, and Lige sighed.

"I never hit anything with my first shot before," Lige said, thinking about the deer.

"Likely you've grown to regard life as more serious business."

"Zeke, you ever have to do somethin' difficult when you were fourteen? Like kill a bear?"

"Had to tend the folks at the big house."

"Tend 'em?"

"They called it bein' an attendant. Just a fancy way o' sayin' I was their fetch boy."

"Was it hard work? Dangerous?"

"Not so dangerous. Hard? Yes, it was. It's always a trial to do a thing that doesn't come natural. Shootin' a gun's that way for you."

"No, it's not."

"Don't be lyin' to me, Lige. You got to think a long time 'fore you pull that trigger. It's a good sign in a man. Killin' shouldn't come easy."

"It's not that hard for a Comanche."

"I expect some o' them find it tough to do."

"I wouldn't care much for bein' a Comanche. I don't think I could do it, ridin' all day, shootin' and burnin' and such."

"There's more to it than that. All this raidin' is on account they had to give up their old hunting grounds an' move. They can't live off the reservation stocks."

"I suppose. Still, I guess I'd be dead already if I'd been born a Comanche. I'd likely fall chasin' buffalo. If not, there'd be somethin' else. I never seem to do anything right."

Lige spread out his blankets and lay between them. The sky seemed suddenly cold, and he felt terribly alone. It hadn't been that way when Zeke's voice was thundering through the clearing. Now it did.

I wonder why he can appear so close one minute and so far off the next, Lige asked himself. But it was impossible to figure people. Lige closed his eyes and let the weariness flow through his body and take possession of him.

They arrived at Red River Crossing the following day. It wasn't much of a settlement, just a motley collection of drifters and vagabonds, crippled Confederates tending shop and traders awaiting news that the Indians had appeared on the opposite bank of the river. When Zeke climbed down from the wagon, a group of traders gathered around.

"You bring goods up from the Trinity?" one of the traders asked. "Want to do business 'cross the river? Old Hazen's a good Cherokee speaker. Grable talks fair with the Seminoles."

"I'll speak to 'em my own self," Zeke said.

"And what about him?" another trader asked, pointing at Lige. "You can't be plannin' to take him."

"He sort of takes himself," Zeke said.

"Seems strange," the first trader said. "A black man an' his white boy."

"I'm nobody's boy," Lige said, stepping forward.

"Sure you are," the first trader continued. "We all know this one. He's Jackson. He traded horses with the Kiowas down to Belknap. I watched him tradin' with Comanches once a couple o' years back."

"He does good business with the Indians," someone added.

"Likely sold 'em guns to raid the settlements. You got guns on those pack animals, Jackson? Maybe to trade 'em so they can scalp us, too?"

The traders closed in all around Zeke, and Lige fought to get between them. Finally, in desperation, he screamed, "You fools, let him be!"

The others drew back as Lige produced his grandfather's pistol.

"I came out here tryin' to bring back my brother and other captives," Lige said, shaking with rage. "All of us along the Trinity pitched in goods to trade for our people. You harm Zeke Jackson, we'll never get anyone back. Understand?"

The men mumbled among themselves. Finally one of them turned to Lige and asked, "How come you ride with Jackson?"

"He knows the tribes," Lige said. "He speaks their language. And I trust him."

The men looked at one another nervously. Finally one of them spoke up. "I guess we'd best leave you to go your own way," the man said.

It took the rest of the afternoon and half the night to

satisfy Zeke that all was ready for the long journey into the Nations. A little before sunset Zeke swapped some cornmeal for what appeared to be a bundle of buckskin rags. As they lay on their blankets that night, Lige found himself smiling.

"See there, Zeke," Lige whispered, "you needed a little help after all. An' I got you through it."

"Sure did," Zeke said. "Now get yourself some rest. I don't want you sleepin' in the saddle like that first night. Not with you totin' that cannon of a pistol."

Lige laughed. Then he closed his eyes and fell asleep.

# 8

Crossing the Red River was a treacherous proposition, especially in the summer. The water wasn't deep, but dangerous bogs of quicksand lurked everywhere. The going was slow and tedious. Lige led Skeeter through the deep mud, watching as Zeke followed a zigzag course across the bottoms.

"I once saw a man an' rider both just sink into this place an' disappear," Zeke said as they splashed through the shallow channel. "Was just like the earth reached out an' took them under. Never saw another thing like it."

Lige's hands trembled. He could imagine long fingers of muck closing in on his feet, dragging him under, covering his nose and mouth until he could no longer breathe.

"But that's nothin' to what's on the other side, Lige,"

Zeke went on. "This is treaty land, given over to the Nations for all time. They don't care much for anybody, white or black, intrudin' on 'em."

"We'll have to be careful," Lige said.

"First night we make camp, we got to make you over into a Tonkawa. How're the Spanish words comin'?"

"Fair. I haven't cooked my tongue again."

"Start speakin' now. You got to be used to it 'fore we run into any Comanches."

"*Sí,*" Lige said, smiling as they began climbing up the northern bank of the river. "*Mucho bien.*"

Zeke shook his head and spit on the ground. "Best do better'n that, Lige. I don't aim to spend the last o' my days on a Comanche anthill."

They managed close to twenty miles through the hilly border country of the Nations. As night fell, Zeke made a foul mixture of berries and plant roots. It reminded Lige of stable muck, and he was none too eager to have it applied to his skin. He allowed Zeke to do it only when it was clear there was no alternative.

"I smell like a dung heap," Lige said, shaking his head as Zeke spread the paste over bare shoulders that already seemed dark enough to Lige.

"You are a bit strong," Zeke said, laughing. "Now, the rest o' you."

Lige stood up and slipped out of his clothes. Zeke was careful to rub the mixture in everywhere so that no spots of white remained. When the man's rough fingers dabbed dye to Lige's face, Lige winced.

"Best to spread it your own self round the eyes an' nose," Zeke said. "Be sure it covers everything, even your ears.

Comanches got eyes like hawks. They'll smell out the trick, an' we'll be finished."

Lige followed instructions. Zeke brought out a piece of looking glass, and Lige inspected the job.

"Now you stand out here an' let it dry," Zeke said. "Can't get it wet for a time. Tomorrow you stay bare's much as you can. Let the sun finish the job."

"I'm not ridin' naked, Zeke!" Lige declared.

"Comanches won't mind. But your bottom likely'd peel itself pink. 'Sides, they'll likely have more interest in your hair and shoulders."

Lige stayed up half the night waiting for the strange concoction to dry. When he did sleep, it was far from soundly. The night was full of noise—birdcalls and raccoons slipping through the limbs of nearby post oaks. When the sun woke him, he found that Zeke already had the gear packed and a breakfast fire roaring.

"You built a fire," Lige said, getting to his feet. "You'll give our position away."

"You sound more like ole Colonel Haskell back at Belknap every day now," Zeke observed. "How we goin' to treat with the Comanches if we don't let 'em know we're here?"

"But I'm not ready. The dye . . . "

"Looks just fine. We got to braid the hair, though. You ready?"

"Muriel Dickerson wears her hair in braids. Not me!"

"You would if you were a Tonkawa boy. Don't give me grief, Lige. It's the best way."

Lige bit his lip and consented. He winced as Zeke twisted and turned his hair. The back was hardly long

81

enough for true braids, but the finished product did have an air of wildness about it. Zeke tied two hawk feathers in back for good measure.

"I got these back at the crossing for you to wear," Zeke said, pulling from the mysterious buckskin bundle a pair of deerskin leggings. "These, too," he added, tossing out a pair of beaded moccasins and a breechclout. "They're Ioni, but I'd guess the Comanches'll be fooled."

"Couldn't I just wear my trousers and a vest? I saw some o' the army scouts in trousers."

"You want Comanches to think you been ridin' with the soldiers?" Zeke asked, shaking his head. "Soldiers been shootin' Comanches for the past thirty years. Only one they hate worse'n a soldier's a Tonkawa scout."

Lige stepped into the moccasins, but he couldn't figure out how to get the breechclout to stay up.

"Got to use a belt o' some kind," Zeke said, tossing him a rawhide cord. "This'll do for now. Best leave the leggings for today, let the dye work on those knees."

"I don't suppose I can wear my hat."

"Not if you plan to have any hair left underneath."

Lige grumbled a little as he sat down with Zeke and ate breakfast. After a few minutes, Zeke grew solemn.

"We'll be seein' Indians pretty soon now," the man said. "First it'll be Cherokees, Creeks maybe. Then Comanches or Kiowas. You'd be better off stayin' right here, Lige."

"I'm goin'," Lige said, standing up.

"It's no boy's game from here on. It's pure deadly."

"I know."

"Scared?"

82

"Sure, but my brother's here someplace. I mean to bring him home."

"What if he's dead?"

Lige felt himself shake from head to toe. His stomach tied itself in a hundred knots, and he wanted to be sick.

"They already killed James and Joe," Zeke said somberly.

"But not Charlie," Lige said. "I can feel it. He's nearby."

"Then we'll find him. One thing, Lige. You keep your mouth closed. Don't say a word."

"I thought my Spanish was gettin' better."

"Is, a little. But one slip, and we'll all be dead. Understand?"

"I understand," Lige said, looking at his feet.

All that day and most of the next Lige rode Skeeter a dozen yards behind Zeke. There was no road now, and they made their way along dry creekbeds and granite hillsides laden with boulders. The sun beat down on them unmercifully, and Lige wiped sweat from his forehead, from his bare chest. He might have taken on the appearance of a Tonkawa, but inside he was still Elijah Andrews, and just as afraid as that night the Comanches had come.

As they continued, they saw few signs of Comanches or any other living being. Zeke made camp that night atop a small hill, and as darkness fell, Lige stirred a small fire and sighed. They'd come so far, and yet they hadn't seen so much as an Indian's dog.

"How much farther do we have to ride till we come to the Comanches?" Lige asked.

"Hard to say. Maybe a week. Could be all summer."

"I thought you said you knew where they'd be."

"Comanches? They don't know themselves. 'Sides, Lige, it's not just us findin' them. It's them lettin' us."

That next afternoon three riders rode parallel for a hundred yards or so.

"Cherokee," Zeke said. "Likely lost interest when they saw we weren't totin' trade goods."

"But we are."

"Well, we know that, but lookin' at our ponies, you'd never guess it."

"Shouldn't we put some of the things out in plain sight? Don't we want the Comanches to know we're tradin'?"

"That's an invitation to get scalped," Zeke explained. "Only ones we want to know 'bout the rifles, the liquor, an' the rest are the ones that got Mary an' Lizzie, little Charlie, and th'others."


As the days went on, Zeke redirected their path. Lige soon noticed they were weaving back and forth along a rolling river Zeke called the Buffalo.

"Are we ever goin' to find 'em?" Lige cried out one night at the darkness.

"Hush, Lige!" Zeke said.

"I was only . . ."

"Hush," Zeke repeated. "Can't you hear?"

Lige sat down and concentrated. Something stirred in the brush nearby. It's only another raccoon, Lige thought. But it was something larger.

"There," Lige whispered, pointing toward two cedars behind the wagon.

"Remember, Lige, no speakin' from here on."

Lige concentrated on keeping silent and watched Zeke pull a pistol and follow the intruder around to the horses. A minute later there was a howl. Zeke stepped out from behind the cedars, holding a young Indian boy by the hair.

"Found us a Comanche at last," Zeke announced.

The boy screamed and squirmed. It reminded Lige of the time his grandpa had caught Charlie in his tobacco pouch. The Indian boy spoke a hundred words, all fast and furious. None of it had any meaning for Lige, but Zeke nodded and replied.

Soon the two seemed to reach a kind of understanding. Zeke released the boy, who went scampering off into the woods.

"We'll be seein' Comanches by first light," Zeke said, grinning. "Sleep light tonight."

With that said, Zeke put aside the pistol and climbed into his blankets. Lige did the same, stifling the urge to shout. And as he drifted off into an uneasy slumber, he couldn't help feeling a sense of excitement. Comanches tomorrow. At last.

An hour after sunrise the Comanches appeared. Three bare-chested men on tall brown horses rode together, led by the boy on a smaller pinto pony. Zeke met them with raised right hand. They spoke for a few minutes. Then the Indians dismounted and sat together in front of the fire.

Zeke brought out a blanket and handed a small pouch of tobacco to the Comanche in the center. The Indian produced a long wooden pipe and began stuffing tobacco leaves in its small black bowl. As they smoked and talked, the

Comanche boy dashed around the camp, going through the wagon and inspecting the horses. Lige kept out of the way. He didn't understand the words spoken by the Comanches or Zeke, but it was easy to see they were discussing the captives. Zeke described the captives, using his hands, touching his face to show some were black-skinned. Finally the Indians rose from their places. As they rode away, Lige walked slowly to Zeke's side.

"Well?" Lige asked.

"They knew about the raid," Zeke said, walking back to the horses. "They say the one to smoke with is an old man named Sky Eagle. His lodge is upriver a way."

"So we're going there?"

"Lige, I guess maybe you should know. They say there's no blond boys up there."

"They could be wrong."

"Have been before. But I wouldn't count on it this time. They seemed to know too much about that raid to've stayed home."

Lige felt his heart sink to his toes. They hurriedly packed their goods onto the horses and got into motion.

By midafternoon they reached Sky Eagle's camp, a cluster of lodges made from buffalo hides stretched over a framework of pine poles. Zeke pulled to a stop near a grove of tall oaks three or four hundred yards from the Comanche camp. He waved for Lige to stay there, then walked on ahead alone.

Lige stared as the tall black man entered the camp. Three mongrel dogs yapped at Zeke's heels, and three small Indian boys circled him, touching his hips with small bows. Soon a tall Comanche dressed in a beautiful white deerskin shirt emerged from one of the lodges. He shouted, and the children scattered.

It was the same as before. Zeke and the Indian talked and smoked tobacco. Nothing seemed to be settled, though. Then, from the river, came a sound that brought a shiver through Lige's entire body.

"Leave me be!" someone shouted. "Leave me be!"

Lige stared as a small white-skinned figure raced through the willows at the river's edge. The boy was naked except for a bit of buckskin around his waist. Lige stepped out from the wagon just as a short, round-faced Indian grabbed the running boy and flung him to the ground.

Lige stood there, frozen. He was afraid to watch, but he couldn't help himself. Three old women arrived then and pulled the captive boy back to camp. It was then that Lige saw his face. It wasn't Charlie. The boy's hair was dark, and he appeared younger.

Is that what Charlie's been going through? Lige asked himself. He couldn't bear the thought.

Zeke returned an hour before sundown. Lige read the somber look on the man's face and sighed.

"I thought the boy . . . I thought it was Charlie," Lige said. "But it wasn't."

"That one was taken near the crossin'," Zeke explained. "They didn't keep any from th'other raid."

"They didn't kill them?" Lige asked, shaking all over.

"No," Zeke said, touching Lige's shoulder to reassure him. "Doesn't mean they're alive, o' course, but there's a chance."

"Where are they?" Lige asked.

"With the Kiowas up to Mud Springs."

"How far's that?"

"Better part of a week maybe. Hard country, too, Lige. You still of a mind to try it?"

"Nothin' could stop me."

"Then we'll be on our way tomorrow."

"Zeke?"

"Somethin' else troublin' you?"

"That boy."

"You want to trade for every captive in the whole Comanche nation? An' the Kiowas, too?"

"I can't help myself, Zeke."

"Well, you got to keep your eye to the job ahead, Lige. No point worryin' over that boy anyway. Ole Sky Eagle an' I talked on it. I figure he'll get that boy down to the crossin' 'fore summer's end, likely trade him for powder."

"But you can't be sure."

"Lige, this is an old game with the Comanches. They been raidin' women an' little ones since the beginnin' of time. For years they raided the Mexicans an' Apaches. Apaches an' Mexicans raided back."

"What makes people do a thing like that, Zeke?" Lige asked.

"No different'n whites raidin' over in Africa. They brought my people over here the same way, to work the fields an' serve their needs. An' they never sold a one of 'em back to their people."

Lige frowned. He remembered the scars he'd seen on Zeke's back. No different, Zeke had said. It wasn't a pleasant thought.

"Don't fret over that boy, Lige. A boy like that, he's not much good to Comanches. Eats more'n he works, an' he whines to boot. Be worth a whole lot more traded for powder an' lead.

As Lige crawled into his blankets that night, he wished he could be sure. And he prayed it wasn't like that for Charlie. Staring up at the stars, he wondered if Mud Springs might not just be the first of many false trails. Would they ever find Charlie and the others? Would they ever get home?

# 9

For three days Lige and Zeke combed the country north of the Buffalo, searching out places Sky Eagle had spoken about. Finally they made their way along a shallow stream known as Rock Creek. It carved its way through the hill-sides, gurgling over small boulders and flowing into a small pond. When the horses splashed through the stream, Zeke motioned Lige to stop.

"Listen," Zeke whispered as Lige pulled alongside.

Lige listened as the horses stamped their feet in the muddy bottom. There was something else, too. More splashing, coming from up ahead somewhere.

"Best to be cautious," Zeke said. "See that thicket?"

Lige nodded.

"We'll stow the horses in there, cover the trail with branches. Then we'll have a look around."

Lige dismounted and led Skeeter into the thicket. After tying the reins to a small cottonwood, he turned and watched as Zeke led the other animals into the trees. Then they began cutting branches and laying them over the trail.

"Now, let's have a look at what's ahead," Zeke said, waving Lige forward.

The two of them crept along the creek two hundred yards or so before pausing. There, on the far side of the pond, an Indian village spread out among the oaks and cottonwoods.

"Kiowas," Zeke whispered, pointing to the markings on the sides of the lodges. "These won't be an easy bunch to treat with. Best go in slow."

Lige nodded. They approached cautiously, ducking into the trees whenever a rider splashed his way down the creek. The approach seemed to take forever. When they reached the edge of the village, Zeke held Lige back.

"You wait here, Lige. Watch, but don't you say a thing. I'll treat with 'em a bit. If they mean to make the trade, I'll wave my hat over my head. Then you bring on the horses. Elsewise, you keep to the trees and don't let 'em see you."

"I understand."

"Lige, don't you go crazy on me if you see that brother o' yours. Remember, his best chance is for me to make a trade. Don't do a thing 'less I tell you."

"I won't," Lige promised.

Zeke emerged from the woods as if by magic. The sight of the black man in the middle of their village alarmed the Kiowas. They gathered around Zeke, pointing lances at him. But Lige could tell they were frightened, and Zeke spoke in a loud, confident voice.

The Kiowas moved back, allowing a short, fat man to come forward. The Indian spread out a blanket, and Zeke sat down at the opposite end. The two then began talking.

Lige could tell from the first the discussion was serious. Zeke wasn't smiling, and they weren't swapping the pipe as before. After a few minutes the Kiowa screamed out something. Two young Indians came forward, dragging Mary Jackson and little Lizzie along with them.

Lige shuddered as he watched Zeke rise and embrace his family. It was hard standing there, cold and alone. The Kiowas had made no bargain, though. The two young Indians led Mary and Lizzie away, and the fat man began arguing with Zeke. The words grew louder. Lige recognized anger no matter what tongue it was spoken in. He almost expected the two men to draw knives. But in the end, they laughed. The Kiowa produced a pipe, and Zeke offered tobacco.

When Zeke returned, Lige asked a hundred questions. One stood foremost in his mind, however.

"Have they got Charlie?"

"Didn't see any of the rest, Lige. They got some of 'em, that's for sure. They wouldn't show me till I brought my trade goods in."

"You're taking everything in then?"

"No, I'll take the rifles and the whiskey, the two black horses. They see everything, they'll know we mean to have 'em all. It makes the tradin' hard."

"I'll help you pack the horses."

Zeke returned to the Kiowa village with the trade goods.

This time three Kiowas sat on the opposite side of the blanket. There was less arguing and more drinking as the jugs of corn liquor were opened. The Kiowas seemed to be enjoying themselves. Lige decided to try to get a better look at the village while they were distracted.

The lodges weren't very different from those in the Comanche camps they'd visited. Except for a barking dog, no one noticed Lige. He crept through the lodges, ducking behind smoking racks or horses whenever anyone approached. As he passed fifty yards from where Zeke was treating with the tribal elders, he saw little Ellen Bailey.

Lige had known her practically from the day she'd been born seven years or so before. Ellen was stirring a kettle slowly. She was frail, more walking skeleton than girl. It pained Lige to watch her standing there in her shredded dress, thin legs coated with mud from the pond, hair braided Kiowa style.

Her father would cry if he could see this, Lige thought. He felt light-headed, wanted to scream or throw something, get back at the Indians somehow. But it would be fatal, and he managed to regain his nerve in time to dart inside a nearby lodge before three young boys ran past.

It was then that he saw Charlie. Lige wasn't sure at first that it was his brother. All he heard was a sudden, high-pitched cry.

"Let go of me!" the voice called out.

Lige stared through the open front of the lodge as an old woman appeared, dragging a small, barefooted boy along. Lige only needed to see that head of scraggly blond hair to recognize his brother. Charlie was nearly as thin as Ellen, but more care was apparently given to boys. His legs looked sound enough, and none of his ribs appeared to be protruding under the skin of his bare chest.

There were marks, though, small red lines on his back and thighs. Anger welled up inside Lige, and once again he felt a great urge to strike out.

I'd only get us both killed, Lige told himself. Still, it was hard to sneak back out of the camp and wait for Zeke to return.

They'll never beat you again, Charlie, Lige promised as he sat beside Skeeter and chewed some dried venison. I'll see you get back home to Mama and Papa.

Lige waited for Zeke. Even when the sun sank into the hills to the west, the big man failed to return. Lige began to worry. He crept along the shore of the pond until he could see the village in the faint light of evening.

There's nothin' I can do, he told himself. I can't fetch Charlie without help. Why can't I do somethin'?

He stumbled back to the horses with an empty heart. It seemed just then that the world was even darker than before.

I don't know what you were expectin', Lige, he thought as he scratched Skeeter's nose. You imagined we'd just walk up and take 'em, an' ride home together in broad daylight. Well, life doesn't work that way.

Lige sat down beside the wagon and listened to the noise of drums in the Kiowa village. From time to time the wind would carry the sounds of singing across the pond, stirring the trees and scattering the animals. It wasn't sad music exactly, more mournful like those Baptist hymns Emma Kramer sang while hanging up laundry.

He slumped against a tree trunk and closed his eyes. He could still see Charlie, could still see the bruises and the marks on his small back. They brought anger before, but now all Lige could feel was frustration. He was so close, and yet there was an ocean of obstacles keeping him from bringing his brother home. And only one hope. Yes, it all rested on the broad shoulders of Zeke Jackson.

You've got to do it, Zeke, Lige thought as he faded off to sleep. You've got to.

# 10

Lige was sleeping soundly when Zeke came back. The man knelt beside the wagon and touched Lige's shoulder lightly.

"Lige, best rouse yourself," Zeke told him. "I finished treatin' with 'em."

Lige blinked his eyes and tried to focus. The words began to sink in, and he sat up.

"I saw Charlie," Lige said. "He's here."

"I know," Zeke said. "All of 'em are."

"Well, then we can bring 'em back."

"Lige, we got trouble."

"I thought you said you made a bargain with 'em."

"That Kiowa Three Claws's tightfisted when it comes to a trade. He offered me my Mary and little Lizzie for the four rifles, the two horses, and all the corn liquor that's left."

"What about Charlie and the others?"

"He won't deal for 'em. They belong to some chief, a real wildcat named Painted Crow."

"Where is he? Maybe he'll agree to . . . "

"There's no treatin' with that one, Lige. He's still raidin'. The Kiowas say he's got the dark eyes. He's mean. You wouldn't want to cross paths with him. Even the young bucks shake when his name gets mentioned."

"We're not leavin' here without Charlie."

"Thought that's how you'd see it. I got myself a plan, Lige, a way to cheat ole Painted Crow out o' his captives. But it's plenty dangerous."

"Tell me."

"Everything depends on you, Lige. You understand? It won't be easy, not a bit of it."

"I didn't expect it to be."

"We'll do it this way. Wait till nightfall. I'll have the menfolk down there makin' our bargain, dancin' an' singin'. You can circle the village till you get to the horses. They're all back in a little box canyon. If you can get the horses off down the valley, the men'll spend their time lookin' for 'em. Might give you a chance to get th'others up the creek."

"Won't they have guards?"

"Seems likely."

"I'll have to shoot them, I guess."

"Whatever you do, don't you use that cannon o' yours. Shot'll alert 'em all. No, figure out somethin' else."

"An' you'll get Charlie and the rest to the wagon."

"No. Lige, you'll have to get 'em word this mornin' while I'm makin' the deal with Three Claws. See if you can get to Mary. Or Miz Bailey. She's steady in a tight spot, too. Tell 'em to head for the horses soon's the drums start. One or two at a time, too. Don't want the Kiowas to catch on."

"I understand what to do."

"Lige, you got to promise me somethin'."

"Anything."

"Once you set those horses to runnin', you got to get back to our camp an' get everybody together. Then hightail it up the creek an' make due south for the Buffalo."

"Where will you be?"

"I got to keep the Kiowas happy. I'll slip off after a time."

"Where should we wait for you?"

"Boy, can't you hear what I'm sayin'? Don't you wait for me or anythin' else. You move south fast as you can."

"But . . ."

"Lige, there's no other way."

"Zeke, you could make the deal for Mary and Lizzie. The three of you could leave. Then we could make our try."

"Too many Kiowas around, Lige. You wouldn't get more'n five miles 'fore they had the whole mess o' you."

"They won't be in much of a mood to let you go when they figure out what's happened."

"By then I'll be gone, Lige. I don't plan to stay for my own funeral, if you see what I mean."

"I don't see how you can get away."

"I plan to leave one o' the stallions tied in the woods. It'll be tight, but I got a better chance than you got o' lettin' all the horses go before some buck plants a knife in you."

Neither thought particularly built Lige's confidence.

That morning, while Zeke confirmed the agreement

with Three Claws and the rest of the Kiowas, Lige sneaked back into the village and sought out Mary.

"You know what to do?" Lige asked after explaining the plan.

"Best tell Miz Bailey, Lige. She'll be in the far lodge, the one with the black bird on the side."

"Remember, when the drums start," Lige said as he left.

Mrs. Bailey was like a rock. She was busy supervising a dozen cooking fires. Ellen was grinding corn while a Kiowa woman was cutting strips of meat from a deer carcass. The captive children sat in a half circle, huddling together for protection from the Kiowa children. The old woman who'd been dragging Charlie around the day before walked through them all, mumbling and shaking a stick.

Lige slipped over to Painted Crow's lodge and darted inside. It was empty, and Lige struggled to catch his breath. He hoped Mrs. Bailey would come in, but no one did. Finally he took a small pebble and tossed it toward the cooking fires. It was aimed at Mrs. Bailey, but it struck the old Kiowa woman instead.

The old woman attacked little Travis Bailey, whacking him solidly. Charlie got a little kick. But while the woman was distracted, Lige managed to get Mrs. Bailey's attention.

"Lige Andrews?" Mrs. Bailey said, recognizing him in spite of the disguise. "What wind blew you here? You're a sight for sore eyes, you are indeed."

"I can't stay long," Lige said. "Zeke's got a plan for gettin' you all out."

Lige laid out all the details of the plan. Mrs. Bailey nodded for a time. Then she frowned.

"Appears like a good way to get all of you killed," she said. "We might could get the children out. But all of us? I don't know, Lige. Seems to me a mite chancy."

"Would you rather stay here?" Lige asked.

"'Course not. For myself, I had a good life. If I die tonight, I got few regrets. No, I was thinkin' you and Zeke might stand a better chance without takin' me."

"Travis won't ever go without you," Lige said. "Besides, I wouldn't know what to do with a herd o' kids."

"Well, we'd best try it your way," she said, smiling. "Now you wait here a second while I get their attention. Then you get clear of this place, Lige."

He wanted to object, longed to talk a moment with Charlie. But getting caught in Painted Crow's lodge would end everything. He nodded his head.

Mrs. Bailey went to the fire and started to stir a kettle. Instead she let the pot slip into the fire. Hot steaming liquid flew into the air, landing all over a young Kiowa sitting nearby.

The man howled in pain. He flew into a rage and screamed at Mrs. Bailey. Other Kiowas rushed to the scene, and Lige was able to slip away unnoticed.

Zeke returned a little before noon, and they sat together in silence. Dark clouds gathered overhead, and soon the downpour began.

"That'll help," Zeke said. "Thunder makes a good stampede. No moonlight'll help the women and little ones get away."

Lige was more concerned that they might have a tough time getting through the muddy creek bottom, but that didn't worry Zeke. And as dusk came a little early because of the storm, Zeke took the last of the liquor and started toward the Kiowa encampment.

"Just you remember one thing, Lige," Zeke said as he started off. "Like ole Lot's wife in the Bible, don't you look back. 'Cause whatever happens, it happens. You just get my Mary an' Lizzie back to Texas. Promise?"

"I promise," Lige said. And as he watched Zeke approach the village, Lige hoped it was a promise that could be kept.

# 11

Under the cover of darkness, Lige crept along the fringes of the Kiowa village. He tried to recall everything Zeke had told him, where the guards might be, how far it was to the box canyon. But it was enough just to get through the dense underbrush without attracting attention.

He wished there was a hint of moonlight to guide him on his way. But Zeke was right. The darkness would be a blessing. It would mask their movements, shield them from the sharp eyes of the Kiowas.

He tripped over the stump of a cedar tree and tumbled to the ground. As he sat on the damp earth, rubbing the scrape in his bare left shin, he wished he didn't feel so defenseless. He'd left the Colt back with the horses, afraid of an accidental discharge or the temptation to save himself from danger at the expense of the others.

He was armed only with the sharp steel hunting knife he'd brought from Uncle Henry's. And, as Zeke might have said, with his West Texas wits.

Lige got back to his feet and set out again. This time he carried the knife in his right hand, ready to use if forced to. It worried him some. He'd never used a knife on anything that was still living, just to skin animals and fillet fish. And even then it hadn't been easy. He thought back to the day he'd stood beside Zeke, stripping the hide from the dead deer. What had Zeke said? It wasn't in his nature.

Does that make me a coward? Lige asked himself. It was a terrible thing to be wondering as he walked into the midst of so much danger. Oh, he could still escape easily enough, but what about the others—Charlie and the Baileys, Mary and Lizzie Jackson? Not to mention Zeke.

Lige remembered the long red marks on Charlie's back. Anger boiled up inside him, and he gripped the knife tightly, hoping the rage would somehow take away his doubts.

It's time I found out, Lige decided. And he started forward.

As he wove his way through the trees to the back of the village, the rain intensified. The wind blew his hair back from his face, and the rain stung his eyes. He found it hard to continue. The branches of the nearby oaks lashed his shoulders, and he fell again. Shielding his face, Lige tried to get his bearings. He could make out the strange shadows that were Kiowa lodges. His nostrils filled with the odor of animal carcasses. He had to be near the dump.

How much farther? he asked as he struggled back to his feet. But there was only the wind to answer, and what secrets it might have known were not shared with fourteen-year-olds.

Lige slipped and slid along the soggy ground as he made a slow circle around the dump. The air hung moist and heavy, clinging to Lige's skin, giving him the sensation of being laden with wet blankets.

Twice more he stumbled, catching himself each time. Finally he left the outskirts of the camp and began the long trek to the box canyon.

He hadn't gone fifty feet before the sounds and smells of horses filled the air. He paused a second and stared through the dark evening mist at the faint outline of a ridge up ahead. He had to be nearing the entrance of the canyon. And to confirm it, he spotted three boys close to his own age prowling nearby, carrying Enfield rifles in their arms.

Guards, Lige told himself. Three of them. He'd never be able to get through that many of them. And even if he set the ponies off, they'd be able to put a stop to it.

Lige knelt in the knee-high grass and watched the guards. They seemed to be arguing. But Lige noticed they were pointing at the sky, then at the village. Lige understood. They weren't any happier about being out in the storm than Lige himself. One of the young Kiowas pointed to a tall blackjack oak at the entrance to the canyon, and all three of them started for the shelter of the tree.

Lige followed, crouching low and relying on the berry mixture to blend his face and arms into the darkness. The Indian boys spread out in a small circle and produced a handful of rocks. They began tossing these, crying out and slapping their hands on the ground.

Lige smiled. Gambling. He'd once watched Seth play cards half the night. Lige left the guards to their game of chance and slipped along the high rock wall of the canyon. Once among the horses, he relaxed.

"Easy, boys," he whispered, stroking an occasional nose as he went. The horses stamped nervously as thunder resounded off the walls of the canyon.

It won't be difficult to stampede them, Lige thought. There was nothing like a thunderstorm to spook horses. He moved cautiously through the herd, shuddering each time the sky exploded with a blast of lightning. Plow horses would already have scattered to the four winds, but not these ponies.

When Lige reached the rear wall of the canyon, he took a piece of hard flint from his pocket and struck it against the steel of his hunting knife. The sparks that flew out failed to disturb the ponies. And the grass was too wet to catch fire.

What now? Lige asked as the canyon walls rumbled with thunder.

As he sat staring at the horses, he recalled something his grandpa had told him once, how he'd stampeded twenty Indian ponies by waving a blanket as he rode by on his horse. But Lige had no horse and no blanket.

I do have my shirt, he thought, touching the rough buckskin fabric. And a horse shouldn't be a problem. There must have been a hundred ponies right in front of him.

Lige took a deep breath and slipped out of the shirt. It was damp from the rain and his sweat, but it would do. As for a horse, Lige picked out a dark mustang that blended into the shadows like a ghost.

In a few seconds he was atop the horse. In half a minute he was slapping his shirt against the horse's flanks and racing among the other ponies, whistling and shrieking. Combined with the thunder and lightning, the commotion started the horses bolting toward the mouth of the canyon.

"Ayyyy!" Lige screamed, again and again.

The boys at the mouth of the canyon scattered as the ponies rushed forward. There was no time for them to grab their rifles or anything else. Lige hugged the neck of the black horse as he guided it among the others, waving his shirt at the stragglers, accelerating their panic.

It took no more than a few minutes for Lige to scatter the horses into the forested hillsides beyond the Kiowa village. There were shouts and cries from the guards, and noises from the village.

"It's time we were out of here," Lige said, pressing his knees against the horse's ribs. Soon they were flying through the darkness, breaking out of the brush, and disappearing into the woods that hugged the edge of the pond.

Lige slowed the horse and did his best to maneuver through the dense brush. Finally he abandoned the attempt and rolled off the animal.

"Get going, boy!" Lige yelled, slapping the rump of the pony. As the horse raced off, Lige slipped the shirt back over his bony shoulders. Then he started for the wagon.

Behind him, the Kiowa village was in chaos. Men, women, and children raced about like frightened rabbits. The noise from the storm drowned out their cries.

Something stirred in the woods ahead, and Lige froze.

He scanned the ground, searching for some sign of movement.

For a moment there was nothing but another shadow amidst a sea of shadows. Then he saw it, a wisp of blond hair, a bare bit of pale flesh revealed by a flash of lightning.

"Charlie?" Lige called out.

There was a rush from the underbrush. Then Lige's brother bounded out of the darkness and collapsed in his arms.

"Well, Lige, you surely did stir up a hornet's nest back there," Mrs. Bailey said, appearing with the others as Lige's arms closed in around Charlie's thin chest. "I think we'd best be movin'."

"It isn't far," Lige said, taking Charlie's hand and leading the way.

"Lige?" Charlie asked as the lightning illuminated their little group. "You look like . . . "

"I know," Lige said, grinning. "Zeke's idea. I'm supposed to be a Tonkawa."

"We'd be pleased to hear the story another time," Mrs. Bailey said. "Just now we'd best get clear o' this creek."

Lige nodded and sped up his pace. When they reached the thicket, he was relieved to see Mary and Lizzie Jackson were already there.

"I knew Papa'd send somebody," Charlie said, leaning his small head against Lige's side. "I just knew."

Lige squeezed the small boy's shoulders, sighing as he realized how frail they'd become. Mrs. Bailey counted heads. Then everyone pitched in and began removing the limbs blocking the trail. Once the path was clear, Mrs. Bailey and Mary helped Lige ready the horses. Mary pulled Lizzie up in front of her, and Mrs. Bailey did the same with Ellen. Lige led Travis Bailey and Charlie to the other two animals, then pointed the way down the creek.

"When's Zeke comin'?" Mary asked as she prepared to lead the way.

"He's not," Lige said, taking the Colt from its hiding place and checking the chambers.

"What you mean, Lige Andrews?" Mary demanded.

"He's back there," Lige said, pointing to the village. "He's keepin' the Kiowas distracted."

"He's bound to get himself killed," Mrs. Bailey said. "Painted Crow'll be back tomorrow. He won't take kindly to havin' us disappear."

Lige shivered. Even Charlie's thin arms wrapped around Lige's elbow failed to chase away the feeling of gloom that was creeping over him.

"Listen," Mary said then.

As the others grew silent, Lige heard the unmistakable sound of horse's hooves splashing in the creek nearby.

"Charlie, you mind what the ladies tell you," Lige said.

The little boy nodded. Travis Bailey pulled himself onto his horse's back, and Charlie did the same.

"There's someone coming," Lige explained to Mary and Mrs. Bailey. "I'd best tend to them."

"Might be Zeke," Mary said, a faint glimmer of hope shining in her bright brown eyes.

Not on horseback, Lige thought, stuffing the pistol in the thin belt around his waist. He gave a last, nervous glance at Charlie and the others, then loosened Skeeter's reins from a nearby oak. Lige threw his damp blanket over the horse's back, then put the saddle on top.

"Just follow the creek till you reach the river," Lige said. "Then find a crossin' and head south. You're bound to reach the Red River. Once across, you're back in Texas. There'll be those who can help you there."

"Lige?" Charlie asked.

"Just keep goin' south," Lige said, choking on the words. "South!"

Lige tightened the cinch, nodded to Mary, then led Skeeter toward the creek and the unknown horseman.

The other horses splashed over the wet and rocky ground, making as much noise as the thunderclouds all around them. The noise upriver grew louder, too. Lige began to pick a lone figure out of the shadows, a tall Kiowa carrying a long lance.

You won't be stoppin' them, not now, Lige thought, glancing around the ground. There was nothing there that would be of help. The Indian detected the sounds of the horses and continued through the water.

He's seen them, Lige realized. It seemed impossible that after coming so far, getting so close to success, it should all be for nothing. He picked up a flat stone and threw it into the creek. The resulting splash distracted the rider. He turned away from the others and moved toward Lige.

Lige replaced his knife in its scabbard and took the pistol from his belt. He pulled back the hammer until it clicked once, then twice. As the rider appeared before him, Lige squeezed the trigger. Nothing happened.

"Wet powder," Lige grumbled as the Indian raised a lance and raced forward. Lige rolled over a boulder and ducked as the lance pierced the air not three inches from his ear. There was no time to think. Lige stared ahead as a flash

109

of lightning illuminated the landscape. A low branch hung across a narrow foot trail. Gathering all his courage and what energy remained, Lige made a break for it.

There was no chance to look back. Lige could sense the lance probing for his back, could feel the pounding of the horse's hooves on the rocky ground. He ducked as he came to the limb, then dove into the prickly plum bushes beyond.

As Lige felt the jagged thorns of the bushes scratch and tear at him, he heard a terrible thump. The Indian had not seen the limb, and it had clubbed him across the chest.

Lige struggled to his feet and stared at his pursuer. The man's eyes were glazed, and there was a great bruise on his bare chest. Lige considered leaving it at that, but the Kiowa regained his senses and stood up. Lige felt around for his pistol. Perhaps the powder in the second chamber was still dry. But the gun was nowhere to be found. He took his knife instead and turned toward the Kiowa.

The Indian grinned as he stared at Lige. The tumble had scraped away flesh, revealing Lige's pale skin in the faint intermittent light offered by the lightning.

"Come on," Lige called out. "I'm not runnin' this time."

The Kiowa pulled his own knife and began turning a slow circle around Lige. Lige matched the Indian's movements. Suddenly Lige realized his enemy did not need to attack. Help would soon come. No one would arrive to aid Lige.

"All right," Lige said, gazing at his enemy with hard eyes. "Come on. Let's get it over with."

Lige remembered the taunting look of the Comanche the night of the raid. Well, there was no hiding this time. He wasn't looking for any oak trees. He was ready to stand his ground, even if it meant dying.

There was a special power that came from knowing he had no chance. The power turned to recklessness, and Lige dove forward with an abandon he'd never known. The Kiowa was caught by surprise. Lige's knife struck the Indian in the side, ripping a long gash from under the left arm down to his hip.

The Indian groaned and fell away, but not before striking Lige a glancing blow to the forehead. Lige felt the trickle of warm blood running down the side of his face.

"So, you've killed me!" Lige shouted, readying himself for another attack. But the Indian remained on the ground, clutching his side and moaning.

Lige felt faint. The knife fell from his fingers, and his vision blurred. His forehead was on fire. But when he touched the wound, he discovered the flow of blood was slowing. He had survived.

For a moment Lige stood there, somehow frozen. He tried not to look at the wounded Kiowa. It was difficult to feel anger now, seeing the agony written on the man's face. I was wrong about killing, Lige thought. It's not so hard. It's knowing you did it that's the tough part.

Lige started toward the Indian. Fear filled the Kiowa's eyes, and he groped blindly for a weapon. There was a noise from the direction of the village, and Lige stopped. Any minute others might arrive. He dared not linger.

Lige felt around on the ground again for his pistol. When he located it, he sprinted back to the thicket where Skeeter stood prowling the ground. He pulled an old shirt from his saddlebag and tore a strip from it. Then he bound the wound on his head and prepared to mount.

They're safe now. Lige sighed, glancing over his shoulder at the Kiowa camp. Lige could no longer hear horses splashing through the creekbed. But neither could he hear singing in the Kiowa village.

I know you meant to swap your life for theirs, Zeke, Lige thought, but it's not right. You've got Mary and Lizzie to look after. Me, I've got nobody.

And so Lige approached the Kiowa camp slowly, keeping to the shadows, blending into the darkness as before. The storm lost its fury, and a quarter moon darted in and out of the clouds.

Lige tucked the pistol in what remained of his belt and stared ahead at the village. A large fire burned near the edge of the pond. Tied to a nearby tree was Zeke Jackson.

## 12

The Kiowa village was astir. Indians stumbled around, grumbling about this and that. Lige didn't understand any of the words, but the anger was plainly directed at Zeke. It took no great imagination to figure what might be in store for the big man. Three Indians sat around the fire, sharpening lances and talking grimly.

There was no way of getting across the clearing to Zeke without being seen. Lige saw that at once. The sole chance lay in coming from the pond, creeping in behind the shadow of the tree. He wished he hadn't left his knife back in the clearing. But he lacked the nerve to go back and get it. Instead he dismounted, took the piece of flint, and struck it on a nearby granite rock. The softer flint gave way until a sharp point began taking shape.

The Indians used to make their spearheads this way, Lige remembered his grandfather had told him. But even with the sharpened flint to cut Zeke's bonds, Lige still had to get to the man. And then there was the task of making good their escape.

Lige thought about it for what seemed like forever. His eyes grew heavy from the day's exertions. He longed for the comfort of the soft straw of Uncle Henry's loft. It would be so easy to jump on Skeeter and ride south.

Now that the storm had passed, a chill had come to the air. Lige took the cotton trousers and homespun shirt from his saddlebags and prepared to exchange his Tonkawa garments for his normal clothes. But as he undressed, he thought again of the pond.

If nothing else, I can give Zeke a fighting chance, Lige decided. He kicked off his moccasins and slipped quietly to the edge of the water. Then he took a deep breath, dipped under the surface, and swam quietly toward the opposite bank.

Lige had never been much of a swimmer, but he'd always had a special talent for diving underwater. He reached out with his hands and drew the water to him. His thin body glided through the depths. Only when his chest caught fire, and he could no longer hold his breath did he surface. By that time he was halfway across the pond.

One of the guards heard Lige's head break the surface, but by the time the Kiowa reached the shore to investigate, Lige was once again underwater, swimming toward the bank. When Lige emerged amidst the cattails, the guards were laughing.

They're just as spooked as those horses, Lige told himself.

The tree where Zeke was tied couldn't have been much more than ten yards away now, but the moon had broken from the clouds at last. Its glow and that of the fire ate away at the shadow of the tree. Worse, Lige discovered his swim, the encounter with the plum thorns, and the storm had undone the work of the berry dye. His legs and chest were tanned, but the rest of him was as white as the moon overhead.

He'd come too far now to retreat, though. He owed Zeke too much. An Andrews paid his debts. Didn't Lige's papa always say that? Lige knelt at the edge of the pond, and when the guards turned to look in the other direction, Lige scampered across the muddy ground until he reached the safety of the oak tree.

"Zeke?" Lige whispered as he caught his breath. "Zeke?"

"Lige, you're more fool that I thought possible," Zeke muttered. "I could hear you half a mile away. Those Kiowa bucks must be deaf."

The guards turned toward the tree, pointed to Zeke, and laughed.

"See there," Zeke said quietly. "They think I'm crazy, talkin' to spirits or some such."

"I'm cuttin' your bonds," Lige said, starting at the rope fibers with the flint. "At least you won't feel chained come morning."

"Is my Mary . . . ?"

"Safe in the wagon," Lige said. "I sent 'em all south like you said."

"They won't make it without you to guide 'em, Lige. You best be on your way."

"I'll bet you could get clear if I distracted 'em," Lige said, the idea springing into his mind. "Maybe I can set a fire."

"You got to be crazy."

"No, just thinkin'," Lige said as he cut through the last strand of the Kiowa ropes. "You pretend you're still tied. In a few minutes, I'll attract their attention."

"Lige . . ."

"You told me once I wasn't doin' the deciding. Well, I am now. There's a big black horse back by the thicket."

"He had himself a Kiowa rider short while back."

"Not anymore," Lige said, shrinking back behind the oak as one of the guards walked over. The guard satisfied himself all was well and returned to the fire.

"Lige, it's a long run to that horse."

"I thought you were good at runnin' away."

"Was once," Zeke said, laughing a bit.

"Well, gettin' shot's better'n what they've got planned for the morning," Lige said. "I'd imagine."

"You might be right."

Lige lightly tied the ropes so that they would appear sound to the Kiowas, then dashed back to the pond while the guards were distracted. As he ducked under the water, a new strength filled his entire being.

Once across the pond Lige got into his clothes and tied the black horse to a cottonwood. Then he climbed atop Skeeter and stared at the Kiowa camp. He would have to make a wide circle, lead the Indians away from the creek, and allow Zeke to get away. It wouldn't be easy.

"Lord, I hope those ponies ran far and fast," Lige prayed, looking to the west where he'd stampeded the Kiowa mounts. Tired as he was and still bleeding from the forehead, Lige would be little challenge to an Indian on horseback.

His luck held, though. He managed to make his way through the thick underbrush and locate the rear of the village. The Kiowa boys were everywhere, carrying small ropes for recapturing horses. A few animals had been retaken already, but Lige noticed they'd spent themselves. No, there was a chance that Zeke could escape if Lige could create enough noise to decoy the guards.

Lige took out his pistol and cleared out the damp powder from the chambers. He cleaned and dried the gun as best he could, then poured in fresh powder. There was no being certain, but he guessed the gun would fire. He took a deep breath and screamed out into the night. Then he rode down on the Kiowa camp, firing the pistol and sounding like an enraged buffalo.

The Kiowas responded immediately. Half a dozen men raced out of the lodges, firing rifles into the air and cursing the intruder. Lige hugged Skeeter's great sweaty neck and fired off his last round. Then he turned the horse and prayed the animal could find wings to fly them away from trouble.

Lead flew through the air all around him, splintering branches and nicking lodgepoles. The boys on the hillside, searching for horses, joined in the chase. Lige dodged one by inches, narrowly avoiding the thrust of a lance. Another raced alongside for thirty yards or so before crashing hard against an unseen boulder.

Lige tried to take note of the pond, strained his eyes in hope of seeing a black man running along the shore. But his own problem was more immediate. He urged Skeeter toward the woods, then slowly started threading his way around to the south.

Lige took no credit for the long ride through the woods that led him to safety. He faded off into a semiconscious state after half an hour of riding. It was Skeeter that kept going, somehow smelled the water and got them to the creek.

Lige woke to find himself lying on a pair of warm blankets in a small clearing beside the river. Mrs. Bailey was feeding him broth. Charlie sat at his feet.

"What happened?" Lige asked.

"You got back somehow," Mrs. Bailey said. "That horse of yours staggered in at dawn. Surely looked to be dead."

"Your face was all bloody," Charlie said. "Should've seen the bandage. But it wasn't much more'n a scrape. You bled more the time you fell off the roof."

"Got pushed, you mean," Lige said, smiling as he remembered. Then, glancing around, he realized where he was, recalled what had happened only the night before. Mary Jackson sat beside the creek, her face long and solemn.

"I cut him loose, Mary," Lige mumbled, trying to sit up. "I thought maybe he'd get away. But I guess there were too many of them."

"I imagine you did your best, Lige," Mary said. But Lige wasn't sure, looking into her sad, dark eyes, that she believed him.

"We best get goin'," Lige said. "They'll follow when they recover their horses."

Mrs. Bailey nodded. Mary called to the children. Charlie helped Lige onto Skeeter and took the reins. The others scrambled atop their horses. Then Mary started forward, and they began their slow, tedious journey south.

For a long time Lige kept looking behind them, not certain whether he was watching for a Kiowa scout or a tall black man on a dark horse. The others seemed so happy it was over. All except Mary and Lizzie. It didn't seem right.

"You saved us, Lige," Charlie said as they rode together southward. "You surely looked like an Indian."

"It was all Zeke," Lige mumbled.

"I'd say you did your share," Mrs. Bailey said. "Brought us out o' bondage, just like Moses in the olden time."

"Now we're goin' home," Charlie said, reaching over and touching Lige's arm the way he'd always done, the same as when they were boys out hunting squirrels in the hills. Lige didn't suppose they'd ever be that young again now.

Home? Lige couldn't help feeling it wasn't finished, that something remained to be done. If only . . .

Lige shook his head and closed his eyes. He drifted off into a light sleep. In his dream he saw a lone rider on the rocky trail behind him, a big man with fire in his deep brown eyes.

"Lige, you all right?" Charlie asked, tapping Lige's arm lightly.

"I thought I saw," Lige began to say. But the rest of the words failed to come. There, out of the dust behind them, emerged that very rider, waving his arms and bellowing out so that the very earth shuddered.

"It's my Zeke!" Mary yelled, turning her horse so that Lizzie could see as well. "He's come back to me!"

Lige shook all over as the man approached. Mary and Lizzie jumped down from their horse and raced to greet him. The reunion brought tears even to Mrs. Bailey's hardened eyes.

Lige got to his feet and tried to say something to Zeke. But there was too much emotion, too much feeling. Zeke's eyes betrayed something similar as he pulled his wife and daughter toward him.

"Now we can go home," Lige said, patting his little brother on the back. "All of us."

# About the Author

"I have long been interested in the struggle for survival that took place along the fringe settlements of the Texas frontier," says author G. Clifton Wisler. "One of the most intriguing stories is that of a freed slave who rode north into the Indian Nations to rescue his family and several others captured during a Kiowa and Comanche raid on the Elm Creek settlement. While *The Raid* is not an actual account of this ride, it does reflect the struggles of the early settlers, as well as the Indians' last desperate attempts to dislodge the encroaching whites. I also wanted to depict the tension between the varied groups in a land they all wished to call their own."